THE HUNTER HUNTED

Skye Fargo had stalked quarry many times—but this time he was the one being stalked by an expert. He had never run into a slayer as skilled as Vic Dunn. Now he wondered if even his swiftness and savvy could get him out of Dunn's field of fire.

Finally, though, he figured he could breathe easy a spell. He had made it to a ledge of a butte that was as safe as a church. He yanked his Sharps out of its saddle holster and squatted on the rim, waiting for Dunn to come into sight.

The next thing he knew, he was lying on his back, listening to the faint report of a heavy-caliber rifle.

He lay stunned. He could hardly believe he had just been shot. Then the reaction hit him. His gut churned and he felt like he would retch. He stood up on wobbly legs and tried to get off an answering shot with his Sharps.

But something happened that had never happened before. The recoil of the big his feet and sent the Trailsr the gully. . . .

THE
TRAILSMAN
161

ROGUE
RIVER
FEUD

by

Jon Sharpe

Ⓢ

A SIGNET BOOK

SIGNET
Published by the Penguin Group
Penguin Books USA Inc., 375 Hudson Street,
New York, New York 10014, U.S.A.
Penguin Books Ltd, 27 Wrights Lane,
London W8 5TZ, England
Penguin Books Australia Ltd, Ringwood,
Victoria, Australia
Penguin Books Canada Ltd, 10 Alcorn Avenue,
Toronto, Ontario, Canada M4V 3B2
Penguin Books (N.Z.) Ltd, 182–190 Wairau Road,
Auckland 10, New Zealand

Penguin Books Ltd, Registered Offices:
Harmondsworth, Middlesex, England

First published by Signet, an imprint of Dutton Signet,
a division of Penguin Books USA Inc.

First Printing, May, 1995
10 9 8 7 6 5 4 3 2 1

The first chapter of this book originally appeared in *The Tornado Trail*,
the one hundred sixtieth volume in this series.

 REGISTERED TRADEMARK—MARCA REGISTRADA

Printed in the United States of America

The Trailsman

Beginnings . . . they bend the tree and they mark the man. Skye Fargo was born when he was eighteen. Terror was his midwife, vengeance his first cry. Killing spawned Skye Fargo, ruthless, cold-blooded murder. Out of the acrid smoke of gunpowder still hanging in the air, he rose, cried out a promise never forgotten.

The Trailsman they began to call him all across the West: searcher, scout, hunter, the man who could see where others only looked, his skills for hire but not his soul, the man who lived each day to the fullest, yet trailed each tomorrow. Skye Fargo, the Trailsman, and the seeker who could take the wildness of a land and the wanting of a woman and make them his own.

1859, Oregon Territory,
Where passion bred hatred
and hatred bred bloodshed . . .

1

Skye Fargo heard the twig snap when he reined up on the crest of a low ridge to survey a lush valley below. Other men, less accustomed to life in the wilderness, might have assumed an animal or the wind was to blame. But Fargo knew better. The twig had snapped loudly, cleanly, as it would under the pressure of a human foot.

Fargo took off his white hat with his left hand and casually lowered his right hand to his hip. Without being obvious, he palmed his Colt and hid it under the hat. Then, acting as if he had no idea someone was behind him, he slowly turned his pinto stallion to the left.

A quick twist, and Fargo had his revolver leveled, the hammer pulled back. He half expected to see an Indian. Instead, there stood a young woman whose blond hair shimmered in the sunlight like golden straw. He was so surprised he gaped, and like a frightened doe she whirled and bounded off.

Fargo glimpsed the shapeliest set of buckskins he'd ever set eyes on and legs that went on forever. "Hold on!" he called out. "I won't hurt you!"

The woman glanced back, her golden mane hiding the lower half of her face. Eyes as blue as Fargo's own were wide with panic.

"I won't hurt you!" Fargo repeated, and might as well have saved his breath. She kept on fleeing. He could have shrugged off the incident and gone on, but curiosity, and those long legs, prompted him to apply his spurs. The Ovaro took off like a thoroughbred with its tail on fire, eager for some exercise after many miles of being held to a walk.

Skirting fir trees and madrones, Fargo rapidly overtook his quarry. She cut to the right and headed down a steep slope into a wide ravine. He lost sight of her when he slowed in order to keep the stallion from losing its footing. Not until he reached the bottom did he spot her again, across the ravine, standing between a pair of tall pines. Oddly, she wore a mocking smile, as if she dared him to keep chasing her.

Grinning at her cockiness, Fargo swooped down on her. Predictably, she whirled and bolted. Not so predictably, as he came to the two tall pines, a rope suddenly jumped off the ground as if of its own accord. Fargo tried to stop but he was going too fast. The rope caught him flush in the chest and lifted him clean out of his saddle. He heard the Ovaro gallop on, and then he hit the ground with a jolt, adding pain in his back to the searing torment in his chest.

Fargo lay dazed, aware he had lost his Colt and that his hat was missing. Footsteps crunched, and a pretty face twinkling with wicked glee appeared above him. So did the muzzle of a rifle.

"Got you, by God," the woman declared. "Wait until Pa hears it was me and not one of the others."

"Who—" Fargo croaked, hurting so bad he thought several ribs must be cracked. He tried to prop a hand under him and the rifle muzzle touched his cheek.

"Don't move a muscle, you back-shooting son of a bitch!" the blonde warned. "I've heard all about you. I know what kind of scum you are."

Fargo had to admit that he'd made quite a name for himself and had a reputation most men envied, but he'd never seen the woman before and doubted she knew him from Adam since many frontiersmen dressed exactly as he did. And as for back-shooting, no one had ever accused him of being a coward before. "Listen, girl—" he began, but clammed up when the rifle gouged into his flesh.

"Don't be calling me that!" the blonde huffed. "I ain't no girl. I'm a full-grown woman. I'll be twenty-one next month!" She paused. "What am I telling you for? I should just shoot you and be done with it. But Pa might care to ask you a few questions. On your feet!"

Fargo slowly sat up as she retreated a few steps. He prodded his ribs and was pleased to learn none were broken. Grunting from the pain, he slapped his hat on his head and painfully straightened. "Is this how you snare all your men? A woman as good-looking as you shouldn't have to work half this hard."

Despite herself, the blonde grinned. But she promptly put a scowl on her pretty face and snapped, "Don't talk sweet to me, Vic Dunn. I'm wise to your ways so it won't work. Just poke those hands of yours at the sky and march to your horse."

The name Dunn was familiar to Fargo. They had never crossed paths, but Fargo had heard a lot about the man; a good tracker, excellent scout, seasoned gambler, and cold-blooded killer. Dunn was a lot like Fargo, except Fargo didn't hire out his gun for money. "I'm not who you think I am," he said.

"Sure you're not. And I'm really the Queen of England." She gestured at the stallion, which had walked back on its own accord and now stood idly chomping on a patch of grass. "Mount up before I put a slug in your leg for the hell of it."

"My name is Fargo," he said while doing as he'd been told. "I'm passing through the Oregon Territory on my way to California. I'm not looking for any trouble."

"Too bad, Dunn. You found heaps." The woman stooped and snatched up his six-shooter. "I'm Harmony Britches, by the way. You should know the name, since Abe Decker hired you to wipe out me and my kin."

"I don't know any Abe Decker."

"You're an awful liar." Harmony wagged her rifle. "Climb on up but don't try any tricks. I can shoot the eye out of a squirrel at fifty yards."

Fargo had met enough country gals in his time to take her at her word. She had a fresh, earthy, homespun quality about her, but underneath she was probably as hard as nails and as canny as a fox. The rifle barrel never wavered as he stepped into the stirrups and gingerly lifted the reins.

"You listen good," Harmony taunted. "Now head for that brush yonder, where I left my horse. And take it nice and slow or my trigger finger is liable to get itchy."

A bay had been tied in the thicket. Harmony mounted smoothly, covering Fargo the whole time. She snickered and nodded toward the trail he had been following. "Pa knew you'd be coming this way or up from Yreka. That's why he sent us to keep watch on both trails. From here you can see anyone who comes along."

11

Fargo had to admit she had picked a fine spot to conceal herself, and said as much, adding, "But you went to a lot of trouble for nothing. For the last time, I'm not who you think I am. And I doubt your pa will be very happy with you when he finds out you've ambushed the wrong person."

"I swear," Harmony said, "you are a slick-tongued devil, that's for sure." She motioned for him to ride to the Rogue River trail. "I bet you're quite popular with the city ladies, ain't you?"

For all her bluster, Harmony was too careless for her own good. She'd neglected to take Fargo's rifle from its scabbard and hadn't thought to check him for hideouts or she would have found the throwing knife hid in his boot. Fargo could have killed her if he wanted, but he wouldn't. Her cherry lips and full bosom brought to mind something else he'd like to do, though.

"Yes, sir," the young woman went on, pleased with herself. "Pa will be right proud of me. Being the youngest and all, I have to work twice as hard to prove myself."

"Where are you taking me?" Fargo inquired.

"You'll find out soon enough," Harmony said. "Although I expect Decker must have told you about Grizzly Gulch in that letter he sent."

"Letter?"

"Don't try to deny it. My sister was at the trading post when Decker mailed it and heard Decker talking to Vereen. Lucky thing too, or you'd have been able to wipe us out without us being none the wiser."

This time Fargo didn't waste his breath denying her accusation. He was more interested in turning the tables, and with that in mind he scanned the slope they were climbing. A variety of trees hemmed them in on either side, which was typical of the countryside. Every mountain was coated with trees, every valley had more trees than grass. It was easy to imagine that one day there would be thriving lumber concerns in the territory. Indeed, Fargo had already heard that there were two or three in operation.

One of the trees on Fargo's right caught his attention. It was an oak with several low, slender limbs. He deliberately angled the Ovaro toward them but made it seem as if the stallion was moseying along of its own accord. In order for his ploy to work he had to distract the blonde for a few seconds. So, looking around, he asked, "Say, didn't you forget your rope?"

Harmony Britches took the bait and glanced over her left shoulder.

The instant she did, Fargo seized hold of a limb and pushed against it, bending it as far back as he could without having it break. He let go only when the Ovaro had stepped beyond its reach. The limb whipped around with enough force to bowl over a bear and it struck the blonde on the chest.

Harmony yelped as she went flying. She collided with a small pine tree and tumbled to the ground, losing both her rifle and the Colt. Dazed, she rose on one elbow and looked right and left for the hardware.

Fargo beat her to them. He was off the pinto before she stopped rolling and had his Colt in hand before she rose. "Now maybe you'll behave yourself," he said.

"Damn you!" Harmony hissed. "That was a sneaking, low-down thing to do!"

"And what do you call what you did with the rope?" Fargo said. "Normally, I treat a lady like she deserves to be treated. But you're too old for me to bend over my knee and give a spanking. I'll settle for answers."

"You go to hell, Vic Dunn! I'll never say where you can find my family! You'll have to work to earn your blood money." She stood, her hands held palms out as if to ward off blows.

"All I want to know," Fargo began, and got no further because she dived for the rifle. He dived too, his boot stomping on the stock as her fingers closed on the barrel. She let out a squeal and raised her fingers to her mouth.

"That hurt! You stinking varmint! If it's the last thing I ever do, I'm going to make wolf meat of you."

Fargo should have known better than to laugh at her comical frustration, but he did so anyway. Harmony promptly sprang, catching him unawares, her arms looping behind his legs and wrenching with surprising strength. His feet swept out from under him and he crashed onto his back. Thinking she would go for the rifle, he bent and extended the Colt to cover her. Only she wasn't there.

The feisty blonde had vaulted onto her bay and was in full flight to the west, lashing the reins wildly. She never once turned and within a minute was out of sight in the underbrush.

Fargo let her go. As far as he was concerned, the incident had been too ridiculous for words, a simple case of mistaken identity that had gotten out of hand. He wasn't about to chase her halfway to the coast to get to the bottom of it. Rising, he twirled the Colt into its holster and claimed her rifle, an old Hall's breechloader.

After stuffing the rifle into his bedroll, Fargo forked leather and resumed his interrupted journey. He tried to shut the woman from his mind but kept harking back to the delightful sway of her hips when she walked and the sensuous curve to her lips when she pouted. She had been an eyeful as well as an armful, enough to make a man who had not been with a woman for weeks wish she'd fancied him.

Then there was the matter of Vic Dunn being after her family. Provided she had told the truth—and Fargo had no reason to doubt her in that regard—her family was as good as rubbed out if all the stories told about Dunn were halfway factual. It was claimed the man had spent time among the Bloods and was half Indian in his habits. It was also claimed he had the scruples of a rabid wolf.

The more Fargo pondered, the more he wished he'd gone after the girl. By rights he shouldn't want anything to do with her or her kin, but he felt a hankering to help them.

Presently the spectacular scenery took Fargo's mind off of Harmony Britches. The trail wound down into the Rogue Valley, a winding green belt dominated by the sparkling, pristine Rogue River. This was the sort of country Fargo liked; largely uninhabited, teeming with game, and easy on the eyes.

It being January, there was a nip in the air. Fargo adjusted his bandanna and pulled his hat lower as he came out on the lowland, and a chill wind stung his cheeks. Even in winter the region was as verdant as in the spring. Moss-covered tree trunks, lichen-covered rocks and boulders.

Fargo made for a spiraling tendril of smoke on the bank of the wide river. That would be the trading post he'd heard about, the sole outpost of civilization between the Willamette Valley to the north and Yreka down in California. He spooked a black-tailed buck that bounded into a gully, reminding him of the last time he'd eaten and causing his stomach to rumble. He could do with a hot meal.

The post was one story, made of rough-hewn logs. Near the entrance stood a hitching post that consisted of pine poles lashed together with twine. Four horses were tied to it. Above the entrance hung a crudely painted sign: VEREEN'S TRADING POST. NO CREDIT EVER.

Fargo pulled the Sharps and strolled inside, pausing just inside the door to let his eyes get used to the gloomy interior. Cigar smoke hung heavy in the air, partially obscuring two men standing at a plank counter to the right. At a table on the left sat two more playing cards. Piled everywhere else were trade goods of every description.

"Howdy, stranger," a portly man behind the counter greeted him. Wiping pudgy fingers on a greasy apron, the man came around and offered to shake. "Vereen is the handle. I own this place. Jack of all trades, that's what I am. Bartender, clerk, assayer, you name it, I do it."

"Do you cook?"

"Sure do. Got me a haunch of venison hung in the back if you're in the mood for a steak."

"I'm in a mood to eat the whole haunch," Fargo said, moving to an empty table and plunking the Sharps down with a thud. "And while I'm waiting I'd like some whiskey."

"On the way," Vereen said, waddling off.

The others in the post had given Fargo a cursory once-over and gone on about their own business. Both cardplayers were hulking men in heavy coats and caps. Those at the counter wore cowboy garb and were hardly old enough to be dry behind the ears.

Fargo stretched his legs under the table and stared into the low flames crackling in the stone hearth. It felt good to be able to rest for a while and not have a care in the world. Well, almost no cares. He turned to the cardplayers and said, "Excuse me for interrupting, gents, but I'd be grateful if you could tell me how to find Grizzly Gulch?"

To Fargo's amazement, the pair acted as if he'd pulled a gun on them. They stiffened and drew back, then studied him with renewed interest.

"Why do you want to know?" asked one with stubble adorning his chin.

"That's my business," Fargo said.

"In these parts, mister," said the other hulk, "it don't do to go around asking questions all the time. Could get you in a lot of trouble."

Fargo held his temper in check and remarked, "I only asked one question. If you don't know the answer, just say so and don't lecture me on my manners. That could get *you* in a lot of trouble."

The one with the stubble parted his coat to reveal the butt of a revolver jutting from his wide leather belt. "I don't think I like your tone, mister."

"Me neither, Rand," said his companion.

Sighing, Fargo turned his chair to one side and commented, "Someone should have warned me. I had no idea the people in these parts are as dumb as the trees."

Rand scowled and put a hand on his gun. Whether because he was burdened by the heavy coat or he was simply as slow as molasses, his fingers had barely curled when there was a loud metallic click and he found himself looking down the barrel of Fargo's Colt.

"Whether you live or die depends on what you do next."

One of the young men at the counter let out a whoop of delight. "Did you see, Andy? Did you see that jasper draw? He's greased lightning."

At that juncture Vereen materialized, a bottle in one hand, a grimy glass in the other. "Hold on here, fellas," he said good-naturedly. "I don't want no gunplay in my establishment. Rand, you and Brickman know the rules. Do you remember what happened the last time you forgot?"

Rand's beetle brow creased as he put effort into thinking. Gradually his right hand relaxed and slipped off his revolver. "I remember," he said. "Mr. Decker beat me within an inch of my life and told me to never let it happen again."

"Don't you reckon you ought to listen?" Vereen asked, depositing the bottle and glass on Fargo's table. "Besides, all the stranger did was ask directions. You could try to be civil for once and tell him what he wants to know."

"You be civil," Rand said sullenly. Rising, glowering at

Fargo, he slapped his cards down and stalked out. His partner, Brickman, tagged along. If looks counted for anything, they would sorely like to catch Fargo alone somewhere. Anywhere.

"You'd best be careful when you leave," Vereen said. "I wouldn't put it past those gorillas to tear into you the first chance they get."

"I'm obliged for the warning," Fargo said to be sociable. "Maybe you'd see fit to tell me how to reach Grizzly Gulch?"

"Sure. You go down the Rogue about ten miles, to where a little valley leads off into the mountains. About three miles along you'll reach a creek. Follow that up into the mountains for a mile, more or less, and you'll see Grizzly Gulch on your right. Can't miss it. There are five or six No Trespassing signs posted."

"Someone live there?"

"A man by the name of Leland Britches has a small mining operation going. Him and his family have been up there pretty near two years now," Vereen said, adding, as an afterthought, "Leland is a prospector. Cranky as they come but don't let his bile fool you none. He's all bark and little bite, that old coon is."

Fargo poured himself a drink while the proprietor hustled off to make his meal. He debated whether to heed his impulse to seek out the Britches clan or whether he should go on to California as he'd originally planned. If there was one lesson a man living in the West learned early on, it was not to meddle in the affairs of others. Meddling drew lead hornets like honey drew bears.

Boots scraped on the dirty floorboards and the two young men stopped at his table. The taller had a cleft chin and wore a Remington .44 on his right hip. The other one, who appeared younger by two or three years, grinned and nodded in greeting, his thumb carelessly hooked in the gunbelt supporting his Colt Navy.

"Howdy, mister. I'm Jess Harper. This is my brother, Wesley. We saw what happened, and on behalf of both of us I'd like to thank you for putting that son of a bitch in his place. I've often wanted to do the same myself but Ma wouldn't like for me to get into any more gun scrapes."

Fargo couldn't make up his mind whether the younger man

was bragging or stating a simple fact. "Had a lot of them, have you?" he responded, keeping his tone light so they wouldn't take offense.

"Only one," Jess Harper admitted, sounding disappointed. "But it was fair and square and I shot him before he cleared leather." Jess glanced at Fargo's pistol. " 'Course, I'm nowhere near as fast as you are. How'd you get so good?"

"Practice. Lots and lots of practice."

Jess nodded again. "If a man wants to be good at something, he has to work at it," he said, as if quoting. "That's what my pa used to say all the time. Then he went and worked himself into an early grave when a horse he was breaking threw him and kicked him in the head." The young man took a breath. "Don't know as I mentioned it, but we're from Arkansas. Our pa brought us up here five years ago. We're ranchers," he concluded proudly.

Wesley Harper nudged his brother with an elbow. "That's enough gab out of you. I'm sure this man has better things to do than listen to you flap your gums." He began backing away. "Sorry to bother you, mister. Jess just wanted to compliment you, and when he gets an idea into that muley head of his, he has to see it through."

Jess opened his mouth to say more but Wesley hauled him toward the door. Jess pushed Wesley, so Wesley pushed Jess, and they went out squabbling.

Grinning, Fargo was finally able to enjoy his drink in peace. The meal Vereen served came piping hot and filled Fargo to the brim. When he was done, he shoved his plate back and poured another shot of whiskey. He could hear pots clanking in the back and waited for Vereen to reappear so he could ask a few questions about the state of affairs in the Rogue Valley.

Suddenly the front door opened. Fargo idly looked to see who it was, then tensed as the huge forms of Rand and Brickman filled the doorway in turn. They came straight to his table and Rand leaned on it with fists the size of hams.

"Outside, mister. Now."

2

Skye Fargo had figured the pair were long gone. He'd dallied over his steak and potatoes, savoring every bite after being so long on the trail and having to make do with his own cooking. It never occurred to him they'd have the patience to wait so long. Now, lowering his hand close to his holster, he said gruffly, "The two of you don't know enough to quit while you're still breathing."

"We don't want trouble, mister," Brickman said. "We saw your horse outside so we know who you are. It's important we talk." Shifting, he glanced toward the kitchen and lowered his voice. "And we've got to do it in private. Sometimes Vereen lets things slip that he shouldn't."

Fargo picked up the Sharps and stood. He couldn't figure out how the two men had been able to identify him by the horse he rode. The Ovaro was a rare breed on the frontier, but it wasn't *that* rare. "I'll come," he said, "but you go first. And keep your hands away from your guns."

"You don't have to fret on that account," Rand assured him, "now that we know we're all working on the same side."

Puzzled, Fargo followed them outdoors. They walked around to the side of the building, scouring the vicinity as if they had enemies who might appear at any moment. The only riders visible were the Harper boys, trotting eastward.

Rand placed his hands on his broad hips and said, "This should do." He nodded at the Ovaro. "We didn't figure out who you were until Brickman saw that calico of yours, Dunn. Abe told us you'd be riding one."

In a flash, Fargo comprehended. They had mistaken him for Vic Dunn. Apparently, Dunn rode a calico, which was another type of pinto, close in coloration to the Ovaro but not quite the same. Mistaking the two would be easy for someone not familiar with the differences.

"Decker sent us to wait here for you," Brickman said, taking up the account. "He knew you were due in sometime this week."

Fargo could have told them the truth then and there. But the idea came to him that here was the perfect chance to learn more about the feud between Decker and Leland Britches. All he had to do was play along and they'd fill him in on everything he needed to know. Or so he thought until he asked, "Is Decker coming here to meet me?"

"No. We're supposed to take you to him."

The brainstorm lost some of its luster. Fargo doubted their boss would be as dumb as they were. Once Decker realized he wasn't the real article, there might be hell to pay. "Before I go anywhere, I've got a few questions," he said. "Decker didn't tell me enough in his letter."

"He's paying you a thousand dollars to wipe out the Britches," Rand said. "I don't see what else you need to know."

"Where to find them, for one thing," Fargo said, even though he already knew.

Rand's face lit up like a candle. "So that's why you wanted to know about Grizzly Gulch!" Then he proceeded to give the same directions as Vereen, adding, "Abe thinks you'll be able to pick them off from the top of the north side of the gulch. It's a climb, but once up there you'd have a clear view."

"He has it all worked out," Fargo said dryly.

"Abe doesn't miss a trick, that's for certain," Brickman said. "Hiring you to kill that old couple and their four girls is pure genius."

Fargo hid his disgust, saying, "Not that I mind the work, but it seems to me that Decker and the two of you could handle four women and their parents all by yourselves."

"We could," Brickman said, "but if word somehow got around, the law would come after us. Abe would rather it be done by someone from the outside. That way he can arrange to be somewhere else and have the perfect alibi."

Fargo was impressed. Whatever else Abe Decker might be,

the man was no fool. "Your boss never mentioned why he wants these people killed."

Rand snorted. "Never knew a paid assassin needed a reason for pulling the trigger. But if you want to know, you'll have to take it up with Abe."

Remembering the tidbit of information Vereen had relayed, Fargo commented, "It must have something to do with the gold Leland Britches found. Gold colic has planted more men six feet under then pneumonia."

"Maybe it does, maybe it doesn't. You can ask Abe," Rand said, abruptly defensive. "Now are you coming with us or not? He's real eager to see you."

Unwittingly, Fargo had backed himself into a corner. If he went, there was bound to be trouble. If he didn't go, he'd make the pair suspicious, they'd go tell Decker, and there would be trouble. It was a losing proposition no matter what he did. "I'm eager to see him too," he said, "but I practically rode my horse into the ground getting here on time, and it could use a little more rest. Why don't you tell me where I can find Abe and I'll come out later?"

"He'll be awfully upset," Brickman predicted. "But if that's how you want to do it, we can't argue." He raised a brawny arm. "Go two miles south. When you come to a gravel bar, cross over. A dirt road will take you into the lumber camp, and you can't miss the big house sitting on the hill."

"Thanks," Fargo said, turning. "Now if you'll excuse me, I have a bottle to finish."

"Abe won't like you not coming with us," Brickman stressed. "He wants to get this over with as quick as he can."

"It won't take long once I put my mind to it," Fargo said. At the corner he glanced around to discover them huddled together, whispering. He went inside and over to the counter, where Vereen stood polishing a glass.

"There you are. I was afraid you had ridden off without paying your bill. Then I'd have to hire someone like Rand and Brickman to hunt you down and break both your legs." Vereen said it as a joke, smiling, but there was an edge to his tone that belied his cheer.

"I gather not many people try to cheat you out of the price of a meal."

"Never happened once in the eight years I've run this post," Vereen said. "The few folks who live around here are basically honest, and the strangers like yourself who pass through never give me any cause to complain."

"Is Abe Decker honest?" Fargo asked bluntly.

Vereen's hand stopped working the rag. "I don't know why you're here, mister, and I don't care. But you might as well learn now that I stay neutral in all that goes on. Which means I don't talk about people behind their backs." He resumed wiping. "I live longer that way."

Fargo leaned against the counter. "Let me put the question to you another way: Are Abe Decker and you friends?"

"More like acquaintances, I'd say. He buys his supplies here, that's all."

"Are you friends with Leland Britches?"

"I like old Leland a lot," Vereen admitted. "I like his daughters even more. One of these days I hope to marry one of them."

"Harmony?"

Once more Vereen stopped wiping. "Not her, particularly. But how is it you know her? I got the idea you'd never met any of them since you wanted to know where they live." Vereen's face clouded. "Damn!" he exclaimed. "Why didn't I see it sooner? You must be Vic Dunn!"

"Some call me that," Fargo hedged. He still didn't know if he could trust Vereen or whether Vereen secretly sided with the Decker camp.

"Well," Vereen said, flustered, and repeated himself, "well." He set down his glass, produced a bottle, and filled the glass to the rim. Averting Fargo's gaze, he downed the drink in one swift swallow, then stood there with his Adam's apple quivering. "There isn't a man alive who hasn't heard of you," he said hoarsely. "The stories they tell would make a schoolmarm's hair turn white."

Fargo mulled whether to admit the truth.

"I don't much care for your kind," Vereen went on. "And I don't want anything to do with this feud between Decker and Britches. So I'll thank you to take yourself elsewhere." Still averting his eyes, he spun on a heel and hastened into the kitchen.

22

"What about the meal?" Fargo said. "How much do I owe you?"

Vereen didn't answer, so Fargo slapped two dollars on the counter and walked out. Rand and Brickman were gone. He mounted, turned the Ovaro southward, and loped along at a smooth gait, feeling somewhat amused at his antics. Here he was, sticking his nose in where it didn't belong, all over a wildcat of a woman with cherry red lips.

The trail was well marked by the scoring of countless hooves. Fargo admired the gently flowing river and the rich land adjoining it. One day, he speculated, hordes of settlers and farmers would swarm into the region and another great wilderness would be no more. He'd seen a lot of that in other parts of the country and it always saddened him.

Preoccupied with his thoughts, Fargo didn't notice the riders heading toward him until they galloped into view around a cluster of willows two hundred yards away. He counted eight, all told, and on drawing closer he recognized the bearish pair behind the leader as Rand and Brickman.

It had to be Decker! Fargo realized, and drew rein. They'd spotted him, so trying to avoid them by dashing into the brush was out of the question. Nor was he about to turn tail and run. He'd made the mistake of pretending to be Vic Dunn. Now he would have to accept the consequences.

The tall, powerfully built man at the head of the horsemen had squared his shoulders and was studying Fargo intently. Like his men, he dressed as would any other timberman; in high boots, jeans, a flannel shirt, a heavy coat, and a woolen cap. A dark beard framed his square face.

Fargo leaned on the saddle horn, prudently dangling his hand close to his Colt. He plastered a small smile on his lips as the riders slowed to a halt, then commented, "You must be Abe Decker."

"And you're Dunn," Decker said, his dark eyes lowering to the Ovaro and narrowing.

The moment of truth had come, Fargo reflected. Decker would see immediately that the Ovaro wasn't a true calico and would suspect he wasn't the paid assassin. Eight to one weren't the best of odds, but Fargo counted on being handier with a six-shooter than the loggers.

Decker, however, looked up and grinned. "I was on my way to the trading post when I ran into my two men here. Glad to see you came as quickly as you did."

Fargo could hardly credit his luck. Evidently the average timberman knew as much about horses as the average horse breeder knew about trees. "I met a friend of yours on the way here," he remarked.

"Who?"

"Harmony Britches."

Decker's grin vanished. "Did you kill the bitch, I hope?"

"No," Fargo said while scrutinizing the other riders. They were all big, brawny men like Rand and Brickman, men used to making a living by the strength of their arms, rough-and-tumble brawlers who would fight at the drop of a coin and supply the coin. Fargo had met their kind in the past and knew they made formidable enemies.

"Why the hell not?" Decker asked.

Fargo took a gamble. "Did you say in your letter that you wanted women killed, or did you just mention the family name?"

"I couldn't give you all the details, just enough to get you here," Decker conceded. "What if the letter had fallen into the wrong hands? That's why I hinted at a lot."

"So now you'll fill me in on all I need to know?" Fargo said. "I don't take a job unless all the cards are laid on the table. Helps me avoid trouble with the law that way."

"I didn't know you'd be so particular," Decker said. "But I guess you have a point. I can see where you'd wind up with a noose around your neck if you're not careful."

Fargo was about to come right out and ask why the timberman wanted the family rubbed out when Decker's wool hat did a strange thing; it jumped a foot into the air, like a fuzzy grasshopper. A split second later the crack of a rifle carried to his ears.

At the gunshot, the riders looked every which way while pulling revolvers from under their coats or rifles from saddle scabbards. "There!" one bellowed, pointing at a hill to the east.

On the crest the bright gleam of sunlight off metal pinpointed the location of the rifleman. Again the gun blasted, puffing smoke.

This time Fargo was the target. The bullet whizzed under his left arm, clipping fringe off his buckskins, and smacked into the soil on the other side.

Decker, livid with rage, spun on his men. "What are you waiting for?" he roared. "You know what to do!"

The timbermen opened fire and raced toward the hill. They spread out, some going right, others left, to catch the bushwhacker in a pincer movement.

Fargo bent low over the saddle and flew in their wake. Decker called his name but he kept going. He wanted to reach the person on the hill before the lumber crowd did. From all he'd learned, the bushwhacker had to be one of the Britches. Perhaps Harmony had got her hands on another rifle.

Whoever was up there needed shooting practice. Three more times the rifle boomed, three more times the person missed. Meanwhile the timbermen sent a hail of lead into the brush under the gunsmoke.

Rather than swing wide to either side, Fargo took the slope at a trot. In seconds he was above the timbermen and closer to the top. As a result, he was the only one who detected movement in a band of madrones to his right and distinguished the outline of a horse and rider moving downward. The clever bushwhacker, by fleeing toward them, had picked the one course of action Decker's men wouldn't expect.

Fargo reined to the right and saw both groups of timbermen veer around the base of the hill. About the time they disappeared, he was among the madrones. The bushwhacker had angled to the left in order to stay in the thick of the trees, making for a point where the madrones blended into the forest.

The intervening vegetation prevented Fargo from having a clear look at the fugitive. He gave the Ovaro its head and closed to within forty yards. Near as he could tell, the bushwhacker had short, dark hair covered by a floppy hat, and wore buckskins.

Decker commenced yelling but Fargo was unable to discern a single word. He concentrated on overtaking the bushwhacker, confident in the Ovaro's ability. The horse he chased gained the sanctuary of the forest and plunged in. Fargo had to rely on flashes of whipping tail to guide him in the right direction.

The rifleman might be only a fair shot, but there was no denying his horsemanship. He rode his sorrel as skillfully as any man could, wending among the tree trunks as if born to the saddle.

Fargo glanced over a shoulder once. The hill was no longer in sight, nor were Decker and his men. In a way he was glad to be shy of them although he would have liked to get some answers. Since the man he was after might be able to supply a few, he redoubled his efforts.

For over two miles the bushwhacker tried his best to give Fargo the slip. He abruptly changed direction time and again. He stuck to rough ground. He even barreled into briar patches. All to no avail. Fargo was too skilled a rider, too seasoned a tracker and scout.

Gradually, yard by yard, Fargo narrowed the distance between them. In time he saw the sorrel's hooves throwing up clods of dirt, then he could see sweat dampening the sorrel's flanks. Once he saw the rider's features, but all too briefly, when the man turned to look at him. The face showed no fear, simply defiance.

Presently they came to an open ridge. Fargo closed in. The ambusher saw the pinto pulling alongside and swung his rifle to bash in Fargo's head. Fargo ducked under the blow, grabbed the barrel, and yanked with all his might. He thought to pull the man off balance but he did far more. The rider went tumbling.

Reining up, Fargo sprang from the saddle, his hand closing on the Colt. The man had hit the slope hard and rolled a dozen yards, into a boulder. Fargo ran down, his pistol cocked. The slender figure lay stunned, facing the other way. In order not to get too close Fargo pushed the man's shoulder with his boot and was wonder-struck when the bushwhacker's hat fell off and a glorious mane of auburn hair cascaded out.

"You're a woman," Fargo blurted, taking in her smooth complexion and hazel eyes. She looked to be six years older than Harmony and just as finely built, if that was possible. Her lips weren't as red but they were fuller, more inviting.

She stirred, groaned, and looked around as if confused.

Then she saw him and glared in utter spite. "Well, you've caught me, you son of a bitch. So kill me and get it over with. I won't be trifled with."

"You must be a Britches," Fargo said, grinning.

"As if you don't know, you polecat." She sat up, wincing at a pain in her side. "I'm Melody."

"Do all the women in your family have such odd handles?" Fargo asked, to put her in a sociable frame of mind.

"What's so odd about them?" Melody retorted. "Our ma has a musical disposition so she named us four accordingly. Symphony, Harmony, Tune, and me take pride in our names. Well, three of us do, anyhow."

"Tune?" Fargo said.

"Her full name is Tuney but she won't use it. Hates the sound. So does Pa, but he didn't have any say in our naming. Ma keeps a tight rein on him."

Fargo couldn't resist. "Your mother wears the britches in your family, does she?"

Melody arched a delicate eyebrow. "Harmony is right about you. You're not at all what we expected. Most hired killers aren't half as likable"—she paused—"nor a third as handsome. It's a shame you didn't go into another line of work. Terrible waste of manhood."

Her audacity made Fargo laugh. "I'm glad I'm not who you think I am. I'm looking forward to getting to know you a lot better."

"Why waste your breath claiming you're not Vic Dunn?" Melody said. "I saw you talking to Decker and his bunch. Or are you going to claim you were just passing the time of day and don't know Decker from Adam?"

"I'd never heard of the man until today."

"Then explain to me why you wear buckskins, the same as Vic Dunn?"

"You wear buckskins. But I'd be willing to swear in court that you're not him."

The woman fought to keep from grinning. "What about your horse? How is it that you happen to ride a calico just like Vic Dunn's?"

"Doesn't anyone in Oregon Territory know how to tell one horse from another?" Fargo shoved the Colt into his holster and squatted in front of her. Up close she was even more attractive, her eyes sparkling, her tanned throat rising and falling rhythmically as she breathed. "Since I have no way of proving I'm not the man you think, I'll have to let my actions speak for me. Get on your horse and ride. I won't try to stop you."

"Nice try, Mr. Dunn," Melody said.

"What?"

Melody poked a finger into his chest. "You're trying to fool me. You want me to go riding on back to Grizzly Gulch so you can follow and exterminate my family. But I'm too smart for you. I'm not going anywhere. You'll have to shoot me and be done with it."

"Keep this up and I'm liable to side with Decker," Fargo grumbled, rising. He was at his wit's end. Nothing he did or said would ever convince her he wasn't the killer. Yet if he couldn't gain her trust, and that of her family, he might as well head for California right that minute. They'd as soon shoot him on sight as look at him.

"Why, Mr. Dunn," Melody said, "I do believe I've riled you. You must have thought we'd be easy to trick, us being country folk and all." She chuckled and brushed brush and dirt from her pants, her right hand moving down her leg toward the top of her boot.

"Tell me something," Fargo said, trying another approach. "Why does Decker want your family dead?"

"Hasn't he told you?" Melody said. She wiped a few smudges from her boot, her body tense as if she was ready to bolt. "No, I reckon he wouldn't. He'd be too ashamed."

"Does he want your gold?" Fargo probed, and received a merry laugh in return. It annoyed him immensely, wanting to help and being denied because the Britches were too pigheaded to give him the benefit of the doubt. For two bits, he mused, he'd wash his hands of the whole affair and leave them to their fate.

"Mister, you're a mile wide of the mark," Melody said. "What do you care, anyway? I thought that you're paid to pull the trigger, not to think." She had both hands resting on her boots, her fingers drumming nervously.

"I've tried," Fargo said, and started upward. Unless he somehow arranged a meeting with Leland Britches, it was hopeless. He turned to request one but had to freeze, the question unasked.

Melody Britches had pulled a derringer and had it trained on his chest. "Now it's my turn, bastard," she said. "Make peace with your Maker."

that in eye.

Melody Britches backed a down and had to catch
herself. I "Now that's funny," she said, "and
peaceful in your Vincent"

3

Skye Fargo made no sudden moves. At that range the woman couldn't miss, and he could tell by the make of the derringer that it was a .41-caliber, capable of putting a good-sized hole in him. He watched her trigger finger, ready to hurl himself aside the instant it twitched. It was the best he could do under the circumstances.

Melody Britches slowly stood. Her delight at getting the drop on him brought a smile, and instead of shooting him dead she had to bait him. "So this is how it ends. The high-and-mighty Vic Dunn, paid assassin, is killed by a woman. Doesn't that embarrass you a mite?"

"You're the one who will be embarrassed when you find out you've murdered an innocent man."

"Tell you what," Melody mocked him. "If I do learn that's the case, I'll put flowers on your grave once a year to show how sorry I am." She turned serious and aimed carefully. "Make this easy on yourself. Hold still and I'll shoot you smack between the eyes. That way you won't flop around afterward like a fish out of water."

"You're as considerate as they come," Fargo said, tensing his legs. It was foolish to think he could beat a bullet, but he had to try.

"So long, mister." Melody steadied her hand and was on the verge of firing when a loud crackling and the pounding of hooves erupted in the brush on the crest above. Startled, she glanced up in alarm, pivoted, and elevated the derringer higher.

Fargo glanced back and saw one of Decker's men break from cover. The timbermen were scouring the countryside and this one had been lucky. On spotting them, the man whipped a rifle to his shoulder, sighting on the woman.

Melody and the rider fired simultaneously. She missed, the man didn't.

The plop of the slug slamming into her left shoulder was audible to Fargo. He saw her fall, and drew his Colt a blur. Twice he stroked the hammer and trigger, twice the rider jerked to the impact. The man tried to bring the rifle to bear on Fargo but couldn't. Going limp, Decker's underling oozed from the saddle as if all his bones had become mush.

Fargo dashed to Melody. She was on her back, a hand pressed to the bleeding wound, her face as pale as a bed sheet. She still held the derringer, and on seeing him approach she swung it toward him. Fargo neatly kicked it right out of her hand. "Don't you have sense enough to know when someone is trying to help you?" he growled.

Melody tried to rise, to scramble away. Fargo sank to one knee and shoved her flat again. "Where do you think you're going?" he asked.

"I won't let you have your way with me!" Melody said. "I'd rather die first!"

"Think for a minute," Fargo said, conscious they had to get out of there before more of Decker's outfit showed up. "You figure I'm Vic Dunn—"

"I know you are."

"And Vic Dunn works for Abe Decker, right?"

"So?"

"So if I'm Dunn, why did I shoot one of Decker's men?"

It was so obvious, yet the amazement etching her features showed it hadn't crossed Melody's mind. She stared at the dead man lying spread-eagle below the rim, then at Fargo. "I don't know," she said, grimacing in pain. "You've got me all confused."

Fargo indicated her shoulder. "Let me take a look at that." He bent over but she drew back, overcome by fear and uncertainty. "I won't hurt you," he said, trying to soothe her, his temper starting to flare. Reaching out, he had his hand slapped aside.

"I don't want you touching me! I still don't know if I can trust you."

That was the last straw. Fargo could only abide so much muleheaded stupidity. Again he reached for her, and when she went to swat him, he grasped her right wrist and pinned it to her stomach. She tried wrenching free in a panic and he squeezed her wrist hard to get her attention. "I'm going to help you whether you want help or not, so behave or I'll have to slug you."

Melody's lips trembled, but she quieted down.

Fargo lightly pried at the blood-soaked buckskin, then eased her shoulder high enough for him to examine the exit wound. "You must be carrying a four leaf clover," he said. "It went clean through but didn't touch the bone. And the bleeding has already slowed. You should be back on your feet in no time." He slipped an arm under her shoulders, another under her knees.

"What the devil do you think you're doing?" Melody demanded.

"Carrying you," Fargo stated as he lifted her off the ground. She was heavier than she looked and he had to make sure he didn't lean too far back as he climbed. "I can't bandage you now. We have to make tracks before Decker shows."

As if to accent the point, from the far side of the ridge rose the drumming of several horses. Fargo hurried to her sorrel, which shied until she spoke to it. He hoisted her into the saddle and propped her there while she weakly gripped the reins. "Maybe you should ride double with me," he proposed.

"I can manage," Melody said. "The day a Britches isn't able to sit a horse is time to dig a grave."

Admiring her spunk, Fargo mounted the Ovaro. At a trot he rode to the bottom of the ridge, into heavy timber, and headed south. A gap in the brush afforded him a view of the ridge. Decker and two others were beside the dead man, Decker gesturing as if cursing a blue streak.

Melody also saw. "He'll be meaner than ever now. He hasn't lost a man before."

"How long has this feud been going on?"

"Three months or so. His side has fired on us a few times and we've fired on them, but until now the only wounds have been a few nicks and scrapes." Melody looked at her shoulder.

"Pa gave us orders to fight shy of them. He's afraid of losing one of his pride and joys."

"Then he didn't send you to kill Decker and me this morning?"

"Land sakes, no. If he knew what I'd done, he'd skin me alive." Melody was having trouble staying on her horse. She swayed frequently and had to hold on to the sorrel's mane for extra purchase. "I tried it on my own. After Harmony told me about her tussle with you, I wanted to put an end to the feud once and for all, before he sicced you on my kin."

"You almost got us."

"I tried awful hard, but I was so excited my hands shook. Shooting another human being ain't nothing like shooting a critter for the supper pot."

"No, it's not," Fargo agreed softly.

To throw any pursuit off, Fargo adopted a zigzag course over the rockiest soil. He wasn't greatly worried, since he believed most timbermen knew as much about tracking as they did about horses. Barring any unforeseen events, he hoped to travel about four miles, then stop and tend to the woman.

But they never went that far. Not quite three-quarters of a mile from the ridge, Fargo heard a thud. Melody had passed out and fallen. He ushered the horses to a narrow grassy spot a few yards away and tied them so they wouldn't wander off, then brought her. Melody groaned as he carried her, but that was all.

Fargo gathered tinder and small branches for a fire. To reduce the risk of Decker spying the smoke, he constructed a lean-to first. The wall of interlaced limbs and brush blocked most of the smoke from rising.

With Melody unconscious, Fargo couldn't very well ask her permission to undo her shirt. Since she was liable to try and scratch out his eyes if she woke up and found herself half naked, he chose to play it safe and used his Arkansas toothpick to cut the buckskin.

A check of her saddlebags turned up a cotton shirt, a garment she probably wore on special occasions. Fargo regretted having to slice it into strips but he needed bandages. He cleaned the bullet hole as best he could without having any water to use and wrapped her shoulder tight. Her bedroll sufficed for a pillow.

Not much later, as Fargo gazed on the sleeping woman's beautiful features, the stallion snorted and pricked its ears. Fargo was on his feet in a flash. He put a hand on the muzzle of both horses so they would keep silent and listened to the crunch of vegetation as riders came toward their hiding place.

Fargo spotted Decker himself, and one other. They were west of the clearing, riding south. He wanted to grab his Sharps but dared not remove his hands. The man with Decker posed the bigger threat since he was nearer, and Fargo observed him closely.

The timbermen peered into every thicket, probed every shadow. The near rider veered, coming even nearer. He was looking down low into the brush. Had he raised his head, he would have seen Fargo immediately.

Just when Fargo was convinced he would have to release the muzzles and draw, something caught Abe Decker's attention further west. Decker shouted "Flynn, over here!" and galloped off. Flynn obeyed. Soon the two men were out of sight.

Fargo lowered his arms and turned to discover Melody's eyes fixed on him. For the first time since they met there was no hostility in them, only keen curiosity. "Believe me yet?" he asked as he took a seat next to her.

"I must confess you've about got me convinced," she answered. "Either you're really not Dunn, or you're the slickest weasel who ever lived."

Placing a palm on her smooth brow, Fargo felt for fever. The wound wasn't life-threatening but there was always the risk of infection, which could be. "You're doing fine. The Britches must all run on the healthy side."

"I ain't been sick a day in five years," Melody boasted. "Our folks have raised us proper. We eat good food, get to bed early, avoid hard liquor, and shun men."

"A beauty like you? Now that's a shame."

Melody's auburn hair shook as she laughed without uttering a sound. "You sure are a flatterer, mister. What is your name, if you're not that rotten killer?"

He told her.

"Well, Skye, I reckon I owe you an apology."

"There are better ways of showing you're sorry."

"Like what, for instance?" Melody asked innocently.

Swooping down, Fargo planted a kiss on her soft lips before she could object or lift a finger. He straightened, anticipating a slap, but she stared at him through hooded lids, her thoughts impossible to read. "Call that a down payment."

"I call that taking liberties," Melody said. "And about as worse a case as I've ever seen."

"All I did was peck you." Fargo shook his head in annoyance. For a woman who liked to flirt, she was as prudish as a Puritan. If all the daughters were that way, small wonder she and Harmony weren't married.

"That's exactly what I mean. If you're going to take liberties, you should do it right so the woman isn't left unsatisfied."

Fargo had been about to stand up to verify that the two timbermen had not returned when her good arm snaked around his neck to pull him down. Her kiss beat his all hollow. She smothered his mouth with hers, her silken tongue darting out to dance with his. Her breath, scented like mint, tingled his nostrils. And her hand roamed up and down his spine, eliciting little tingles of pleasure.

"Now that's how you take liberties," Melody said on breaking for air. " 'Course, if you ever took a liberty like that with me, Pa would likely fill you full of lead."

Fargo didn't know if she was being serious or teasing him. He leaned down for another sweet taste but she pushed her hand against his chest.

"Don't your ears work? Besides, when a girl is in agony from a bullet wound is hardly the best time to be thinking about making love to her." She tweaked his cheek, hard. "Keep in mind, though, it won't hurt forever."

Her mixed signals were enough to give Fargo fits. To cool down he moved to the edge of the trees and searched for Decker. For the time being it appeared they had given his men the slip. He relayed the news to the auburn-haired lovely.

"Good. Then it's safe for us to ride to the gulch." Propping herself on her hand, she succeeded in sitting up. "Help me onto Walnut and we can be on our way."

"You need more rest," Fargo advised.

"I'll get plenty once I'm safe with my kin." Melody held

out her arm. "Be a gentleman and give me a boost." She saw that he had no intention of doing so and beckoned with a finger. "You have no cause to worry. The Britches are a lot tougher than most give us credit for being. It doesn't matter that we're females. We can hold our own against a passel of men any day."

Fargo offered an arm, but he wasn't happy about it. She winced as he helped her into the stirrups. He thought she'd keel over but she held her backbone straight and grit her teeth.

"Try to keep up," Melody said.

The sorrel took off at a trot. Fargo retrieved her bedroll and hastened after her so he would be there to catch her when she collapsed. She surprised him, riding without difficulty on a winding game trail that in due course brought them to the Rogue River. From under cover they scanned the main trail and saw no one else.

"I guess it's safe," Melody said, assuming the lead once more. She was pale but determined, the point of her chin resembling the point of an anvil.

Fargo knew she felt a lot worse than she let on. "We can stop and rest any time you want," he mentioned. "There's no use in wearing yourself to a frazzle."

"Do you hear me complaining?" Melody rejoined. "Women don't whine when they're feeling poorly. It's you big, tough men who turn into babies if you get so much as a sliver in your finger. Ma says that's because the Good Lord wanted to balance out the blessings. He made men dumber than women, so it's only fair he made them weaker too so they'd know enough to bellyache when they need mending."

Fargo had a few choice comments to make but settled for, "Your mother must be the philosopher in your family."

"She's the brains. Even Pa would admit to that."

An image came to Fargo of a huge barrel of a woman armed with a meat cleaver and a rolling pin. He didn't envy Leland Britches one bit.

They rode south until the little valley unfolded on their left. Three miles farther gurgled a creek, just as Vereen had said there would be. Melody paralleled it into the mountains, slowing when the gulch appeared on the right. "My home," she said in tired relief.

Fargo thought Grizzly Gulch badly misnamed. By any standard it was more like a gorge; the towering walls were too high, too sheer. The creek meandered into it, first hugging one wall, then the other. A dusty trail, rutted by wagon wheels, never strayed more than a few yards from the water's edge.

Since the Britches had lived in the gulch for some time, Fargo counted on there being a cabin, or at least a shack, and maybe a stable. He put a hand over his eyes to shield them from the sun but did not spot a single structure. "How far back in do you live?" he asked.

"You'll see soon enough."

The sorrel plodded at a snail's pace. Fargo rode behind Melody so the family would see her first. As trigger-happy as the Britches were, they'd probably shoot him otherwise.

Suddenly Fargo had the feeling that he was being watched. Men who lived long in the mountains or on the plains often acquired the instinct. He'd felt it many times during his travels and had learned the hard way not to take his intuition lightly.

Removing his hat, Fargo ran a hand through his hair. While doing so, he secretly scoured the bottom of the gulch. Plenty of hiding places existed. The floor was dotted with boulders, patches of brush and timber, and downed trees. A Britches could be hiding anywhere. He wasn't very concerned. They would see the woman and know all was well.

Then Melody groaned softly, slumped, and began to tilt to one side.

"Wake up," Fargo said sternly, but she continued to sag. Realizing she had passed out, he drew rein, slid down, and reached the sorrel just in time to catch her. She groaned again as he gently placed her in the shade of a boulder. Her brow felt warm to the touch but he figured exhaustion from her ordeal must be to blame. "You'll be all right," he said, half to himself.

"Which is more than can be said for you," declared a raspy voice to his rear.

Fargo started to turn, to stand. He stopped when a hard object was rammed against the back of his skull and there was a distinct click.

"I wouldn't, stranger, unless you're partial to having your brains blown out."

"Scratch your itchy finger, mister," Fargo said. "I'm on your side."

"Who are you calling 'mister'?"

A blow to the left kidney brought Fargo to his knees. Lanced by searing agony, he automatically reached behind him to press a hand to his back. His hand was kicked aside, then he was kicked in the spine. He fell to his elbows and knees, gritting his teeth against the pain, his fists bunched so he could swing when his attacker stepped in front of him.

It was a woman. She had the lowest, raspiest voice of any female Fargo had ever met, but there could be no doubt she was a member of the fairer sex. So to speak. She had the facial lines of a Britches and a full head of rich black hair. Unlike Harmony and Melody, though, she was on the chunky side, with broad, manly shoulders and thick thighs. Her breasts fit her build; they were enormous, like a pair of watermelons straining against her flannel shirt. She wore the family attire, buckskins, only she favored moccasins instead of boots.

"So you shot my sweet sister and forced her to bring you to the gulch," this imposing specimen declared. "Well, you'll rue this day in hell, Dunn. Because it's the last mistake you'll ever make."

"I'm not Vic Dunn," Fargo said. "Ask—" He was cut short by her foot slamming into his ribs. For a female she could kick like a mule. A wave of torment washed over him and he had to gasp to breathe.

"Spare me the lies, stupid," the woman said. "I'm not the gullible sort."

Fargo felt his Colt being lifted from his holster and feebly tried to stop her. She laughed and pushed his hand away. Struggling to control the pain, he slowly rose on his knees and glared at her. "You're the one who is making a mistake. Wait and ask your sister when she comes to. My name is Skye Fargo."

"And I'm Martha Washington." The woman roared like a man and slapped her thigh. "Actually, I'm Symphony Britches. Folks generally call me Sym."

"I'd say I'm pleased to meet you, but I don't like to lie," Fargo responded. He never let anyone lay a hand on him, so to be kicked around by her made him mad to his core.

"Ain't you the spunky one," Sym said, chortling. "I like my men with a little fire below their belts, but I expect you won't be around long enough for us to have any fun." She winked and licked her lips.

Fargo was too angry to fully appreciate her brazen humor. He slowly straightened but stopped when she swung her rifle barrel to within an inch of his nose.

"Did I say you could move?" Sym grinned, then flung a foot in the direction of her sister. "Since Melody can't ride, one of us gets to carry her the rest of the way. See if you can figure out which one."

The walk seemed to take forever. Fargo's shoulders ached terribly after a while but he refused to show any weakness by asking if he could set Melody down for a moment. The trail wound steadily deeper into Grizzly Gulch, past a large dredge and boom. Farther on, at a wide gravel bar in the creek, sat a dragline and a separating bin.

The braying of a donkey drew Fargo's gaze to a high cliff shrouded in shadow. In addition to the jackass, eight horses were penned in a rough-hewn corral. Fargo looked for a cabin but saw only oak trees and a pool situated to the right of the cliff, which sealed off the end of the gulch. There was no other way out.

"Where are we going?" Fargo wondered aloud.

Sym jabbed him with the rifle. "Just keep on, little man. We're almost there."

The oak trees spread out before him. Fargo saw movement beyond the trunks, deep in the shadows covering the lower third of the rock wall. He looked closer and saw that the shadows weren't shadows at all. Erosion had worn a cavity large enough to accommodate a Mississippi riverboat, a grotto of sorts, which served as home for the Britches clan. A grizzled man in dirty clothes was busy chipping at quartz while a woman in her fifties stood at a table kneading dough.

"Ma! Pa!" Sym bellowed like a mule-skinner. "Come see what I've caught."

Fargo was shoved again. He tripped but recovered, then walked on until he was just inside the grotto. Leland Britches and his wife were shoulder to shoulder, eyeing him as they might a lamb for the slaughter.

"You've shot our precious little girl," the miner snapped, reaching behind him. "There's no varmint lower than one who will shoot a woman. And I know what to do with varmints." So saying, he drew a Bowie knife and advanced.

4

Skye Fargo was caught between the proverbial rock and a hard place. Behind him stood a vengeful woman with a cocked rifle pointed at his backbone. Coming toward him, eyes gleaming with righteous wrath, was a man with a gleaming Bowie. And as if the situation wasn't bad enough, he had his arms full. If he let go of Melody to defend himself against Leland, Sym would put a bullet into him. Yet what choice did he have? Fargo was about to release her when the mother of the clan spoke up in a firm tone.

"Don't be killing him unless I say to, Leland. I want to talk to the stranger first."

"Why waste words, Maude?" her husband replied. "It's plain he's the paid killer Decker sent for."

Maude Britches was wiping her hands on her apron. A fine figure of a woman, yet well over fifty, she wore a faded brown dress that had seen its prime years ago. Her features revealed where the daughters got their good looks, except for Sym, who unfortunately took more after her father. "I won't tell you twice, husband," Maude said.

It was remarkable, the effect she had on him. In the blink of an eye Leland changed from a glowering pillar of wrath to a tame wolf ready to jump through her hoops on command. "Whatever you say, dearest."

Maude indicated a battered, torn bed lying against a side wall. "Put her there if you would please, mister. It's not much but it's the only bed we have."

With Leland on one side and Sym on the other and both of them looking at him as if they were praying he would try something, Fargo did as the mother requested. Maude sat on the edge of the bed to examine Melody.

"Did you put lead into my girl?"

"No, ma'am," Fargo answered. "It was one of Decker's men. I returned the favor, so now he won't be putting lead into anyone ever again."

"Most peculiar. We heard that a man answering to your description has come to these parts to kill us. Name of Dunn. Is that your handle?"

"No, ma'am," Fargo said again, being as polite as a church deacon. Whether he lived or died depended on how highly he impressed her and he very much wanted to go on breathing. He revealed his name, adding, "Your daughter Harmony mistook me for Dunn and tried to kill me. Later Melody made the same mistake. Even Decker thinks I'm his killer." Fargo marshaled a lopsided grin. "I guess the only one in this whole valley who knows I'm not Dunn is my horse."

"Too bad horses can't talk," Maude said. She was taking Melody's pulse. "But if what you say is true, we'll know once she comes to. In the meantime"—Maude faced Sym—"put our guest where he won't do no mischief."

"I promise to behave," Fargo said, but could not say more because Symphony marched up to him and jammed her rifle into his stomach. "Walk toward the back, Mister Whatever-Your-Name-Is. And feel free to try and grab my gun if you want. I ain't shot a no-account assassin before. I'm curious to see if you die like a real man or whether you'll beg me to put you out of your misery."

Maude shook her head. "Now, now, Sym. I want you to be civil to our guest until we know if he's a lying dog or not. If he is, I'll let you do as you please."

"Yes, Ma," the big woman said eagerly.

Fargo was steered toward the rear of the huge cavity. The shadows darkened until he could barely see the ground in front of him. To the right were stacked crates. To the left odds and ends had been piled: an old saddle, broken tools, a table with a busted leg, and more. He stared at the wall, thinking there must be a passage, perhaps a tunnel the miner had dug.

Fargo took three more strides. Then, without warning, he stepped into thin air and plummeted. He tried to twist, to grab solid ground, but missed, ripping skin off several fingertips. For a few harrowing moments he fell through inky space, wondering if the Britches had deceived him and seen fit to have him smashed to bits at the bottom of a mine shaft.

The shock of hitting threw Fargo off balance and wrenched his ankle. He tried to keep his feet but fell against a solid wall, scraping his chin. Peering upward, he distinguished the outline of a large hole, or pit, which framed Sym's moon face. Her low laughter made him wish he had a rock to throw.

"If you want anything, holler. If I feel like answering, maybe I will."

More laughter echoed eerily as the woman walked off. Fargo paced the pit, measuring it as nine feet in diameter and perhaps ten feet high. He put his back to the wall, girded his legs, and dashed like mad toward the far wall, hurtling into the air at the very last instant. The rim was a foot higher than he could reach.

Refusing to admit defeat, Fargo ran his hands over his prison, seeking purchase. All he found was a rock surface so smooth a spider couldn't climb it. Twice more he attempted to leap to the top and each time he fell back down again.

Fargo decided to sit and mull things over. His attempt at being a Good Samaritan had boomeranged badly, putting him at the mercy of a gun-crazy family that would as soon put windows in his skull as look at him, and at odds with a powerful timberman unscrupulous enough to have hired one of the most feared paid killers in the West. It was enough to make him swear off good deeds for the rest of his life.

A tiny pebble hit the bottom of the pit with a smack, and Fargo tilted his head back. Another pale face had replaced that of Symphony Britches, a smaller face sheathed in short blond hair. Since Fargo had met all the members of the family except one, he said, "You must be Tune."

The face pulled backward and was gone for the space of a minute. It slowly reappeared and a tiny voice asked, "How do you know who I am, mister?"

"Harmony told me," Fargo said. "Your mother named you Tuney but you hate the name and want everyone to call you Tune. I gather you're the youngest."

"I'll be sixteen in four months," the girl said with all the pride her youth could muster. "Ma says I'm pretty near a woman."

"Your mother strikes me as a nice lady," Fargo said sincerely. At any other time he would have shooed the girl away since he was much more comfortable around grown women than sprouts. But he was grateful for the company. And too, winning her over would give him an ally when the time came for her family to determine his fate. A young ally, to be sure, but he was at the point where he would take all the help he could get.

"Ma is the best person alive," Tune boasted passionately. "She's always treated us as if we're pure gold."

"I just hope she's as fair as she is nice and won't let your father put a slug into me without cause."

"Pa can't do anything without Ma's say-so. Why, sometimes I suspect he asks her how far he can spit before he does."

Fargo smiled and rested his hands on his knees. "What can you tell me about this business with Abe Decker? I've come in on the middle of the feud and I have the feeling I've missed an important fact or two."

"I'm afraid I can't help you, mister. My folks won't talk about it around me and my sisters say I'm too little to know what's going on." Tune sounded bitter. "Seems to me that if I'm old enough to be killed by Decker, then I ought to be old enough to learn why."

"Seems fair to me," Fargo agreed, disappointed he couldn't learn more. No matter how he tried, he was balked at every turn. "Any chance of my getting something to drink? Water would be nice, if you could lower me a canteen."

"I'll be right back," Tune said, scooting off.

Fargo stood to be ready. He was tempted to try to jump to the rim again but discarded the idea as a waste of energy. His only consolation in the whole mixed-up affair was that he still had his throwing knife snug in its ankle sheath in his right boot. The Britches hadn't thought to search him and their oversight might prove to his advantage later.

Footsteps sounded overhead, heavier treads than a young girl would make. Fargo was surprised when two people appeared. One, judging by the size, had to be Sym. The other, he realized a moment later, was Harmony. He grinned at her and said, "Seems like every time I run into you, you've got the better of me."

"Howdy, killer," Harmony said. "Looks like you'll be getting your due soon."

"Not after your sister revives," Fargo said. "Once you've heard her out, you'll have a lot of apologizing to do."

Sym snorted like a heifer. "You might have to wait quite a while for that to happen, mister. Melody has taken a sudden turn for the worse. She's got a high fever and the chills. Ma thinks that wound is infected."

Fargo was fit to curse a blue streak but instead he slapped the rock wall with an open palm. He didn't relish the notion of being stuck in that pit for however long it took Melody to recover. "You've got to let me out of here. I'll find some other way to prove who I am."

"Fat chance you're going anywhere," Sym said. "Now stand aside so I don't conk you on the noggin."

Fargo did, and none too soon. A canteen tied to the end of a rope sailed toward his head. It jerked to a stop a yard from the bottom and swung in circles, spinning wildly.

"Don't stand there like a dumb ox," Sym chided. "Tuney told us you wanted a drink. So get to guzzling or go thirsty."

Snatching the rope, Fargo held it steady so he could grasp the canteen itself. After removing the plug, he tilted the mouth to his lips and drank slowly, dawdling on purpose. He noticed that Sym held the other end of the rope. He couldn't be sure because of the darkness, but he believed she had a loop over one wrist. Harmony held a rifle, angled over her shoulder, the barrel slanted at the stone ceiling. An idea came to him, a scheme he hesitated to put into action since one of the women might be harmed and the mother would turn against him.

"Hurry it up, bastard," Sym said. "Ma told us to give you something to drink. She didn't say we had to spend the whole day at it."

Fargo made up his mind. Swishing the water in the canteen, he stared at the big woman and said, "Too bad you're up there and I'm down here. I like my women to have lots of sand, and I'll bet you have enough to border an ocean."

Sym's laugh rumbled off the walls. "Why, you frisky little runt! You're as brazen as a whore!" She leaned forward, her

45

oversized teeth like those of a heifer. "Any other time or place, I might give you a toss in the hay. Not that I think you could keep up with me, but it'd be fun. I ain't had a man in a coon's age. For some reason most are afeared of me."

"A pretty filly like you? I can't think why they would be," Fargo said.

Harmony fidgeted and snapped, "If you two are done acting like elk in rut, I've got things to do."

"No you don't," Sym said. "You're just jealous because the runt has taken a shine to me."

"I am not," Harmony responded, but the way she said it showed the opposite to be true.

"Are to!" Sym said, chuckling. "Why, I guess you had your heart set on bedding this billy goat yourself, didn't you?"

"No!" Harmony said, too stridently.

Sym straightened and took up some of the slack in the rope. "Shame on you, little sister. You ought to know that you can't kid a kidder. But don't fret. I won't tell Ma. She gets so touchy about us not behaving like decent ladies should."

Fargo had plugged the canteen, which he held in his left hand. His right loosely gripped the rope at shoulder height. "Your mother should be proud," he said, to keep them distracted. "She's raised a fine bunch of beauties." He focused on Sym. "But none of them are as much woman as you. Why, you could probably wrestle a grizzly to a tie."

"Don't think I couldn't!" Sym said, clearly tickled by his flattery. "I can beat my sisters at arm wrestling and I only have to use two fingers to their five. I'm as tough as a she-bear and twice as lively."

"You're my kind of woman. If you were thrown by a horse, you'd probably get right up and give it a wallop," Fargo said, his right hand clamping tight.

"How did you know?" Sym said. "I've been bucked a few times, but it never hurt. Why, once I was climbing up the side of the gulch to get some bird's eggs from a nest and I fell practically fifty feet. Didn't do more than have me seeing double for a couple of days."

"That's what I wanted to hear," Fargo said, his most engaging smile bestowed on them so neither would suspect. "I guess a little fall like this won't hurt you one bit."

"Like what?" Sym said, uncomprehending.

Muscles rippling, Fargo heaved on the rope with both hands. For once things went his way and Sym flew over the rim like an ungainly bird, squawking and flapping her arms. He stepped to the right and crouched. Sym thudded onto her back, raising puffs of dust, as his hand closed on the hilt of his Arkansas toothpick. So swiftly did he move that he had the point pressed to her pale throat before Harmony Britches could react. "Lower that rifle down here or I'll slit your sister's throat," he bluffed.

Harmony had started to level her weapon. She paused, racked by indecision.

"I won't tell you twice," Fargo said. "Your sister is still alive but she won't be for long if you don't cooperate."

"Damn you!" Harmony hissed. She glanced toward the front of the grotto, then back down at Skye. "All I'd have to do is yell and Ma and Pa would be here lickety-split."

"Go ahead," Fargo said. "They can help haul your sister's body out." He disliked having to resort to such an underhanded ruse but the family had left him no choice. He'd be damned if he was going to let them hold him captive. And since they had made it plain they didn't want his help, he'd ride on to California and leave them to the not so tender mercies of Abe Decker.

Harmony wavered, then said, "I reckon you would murder her, Dunn, you buzzard." Kneeling, she gripped her rifle by the stock and eased it downward.

"Don't try anything," Fargo warned as he stood on tiptoe. "I can throw this knife into Sym before you can pull the gun back up and fire."

"I know," Harmony said sourly, so furious she muttered a few choice words about, "stinking, rotten sons of bitches."

Fargo grasped the barrel and she released the stock. Reversing his grip, he pointed the gun in the general direction of Sym's head but not directly at it in case something happened and the rifle went off. From above, it would appear as if he was aiming at her face. "Here's how we'll do this. I'll toss you the rope and you'll tie it to something, then you'll help haul me out."

"There's nothing to anchor it to."

"Now which one of us is lying?" Fargo said. "There's a whole pile of junk up there. If nothing else, you can haul that broken table over." He paused, mentally ticking off things that could go wrong. "Where are your parents?"

"Pa was mad that Ma wouldn't let him put an end to your bloodthirsty career so he went up the creek a ways to do some work. Ma is yonder on the bed, tending Melody."

"And Tune?"

"I don't know. She's like a danged rabbit, always bouncing from place to place and getting underfoot when you least want her to." Harmony looked toward the gulch. "I think Ma sent her to fetch a pail of water."

"You go bring the table. And be quick about it."

The blonde scurried to obey and Fargo hunkered down to check on Sym. The big woman breathed deeply, unconscious. He probed but found no broken bones.

Standing, Fargo stepped closer to the wall, where it was darkest. There was always a danger Harmony would betray him, and if so the Britches would try to pick him off before he knew they were up there. Tense minutes went by. He was doubting the wisdom of his plan when a scraping noise preceded her arrival.

"I brought the table and wedged the busted leg into the ground," Harmony said. "But don't blame me if it doesn't hold."

Fargo lifted the canteen, cocked his arm. "Catch," he said, and tossed the canteen underhanded. It arced high enough for the blonde to seize, the rope streaming behind it.

Harmony was gone under thirty seconds, prompting Fargo to ask, "Are you sure that you tied it tightly?"

"Of course. What kind of an idiot do you take me for?" Harmony said. She wound the rope twice around her waist, once around her left arm, and braced her shapely legs near the edge. "All right, mister. Let's get this over with."

Fargo held the hilt of the toothpick to his mouth as if it were an harmonica, and bit down. He wedged the rifle under his gunbelt, which was awkward but couldn't be helped since the gun had no sling. Now both hands were free for the climb.

It was nerve-wracking. Fargo knew he would be helpless if any of the family popped up with a gun. He couldn't climb fast enough to suit him, and the short hairs at the nape of his neck prickled the entire time.

Harmony strained mightily to support his weight. Often she grunted and dug her heels in deeper. Her body shook, as if she were cold. Twice, one or the other of her knees buckled but she was able to plant her feet firmly again.

Sym Britches was groaning when Fargo gained the rim and shoved to his feet. He unlimbered the rifle, fixed it on Harmony's midriff, then slid the toothpick into its sheath.

"I wondered where you got that pigsticker from," she said. "I thought maybe Tune had given it to you."

Dozens of yards away, Maude stood at a stove, boiling water. She cast repeated worried looks at the bed. Once she gazed into the recesses of the grotto but the sunlight did not penetrate far enough for her to spot Fargo.

"What now, mister?" Harmony asked.

"Walk in front of me," Fargo directed, stepping behind her. He took hold of her elbow and pressed the barrel into the small of her slender back. So close, he could smell the tantalizing fragrance of her hair. Reminding himself to stay alert for the others, he ducked low and guided her toward her mother.

Maude had moved to the table and was skinning potatoes. Within arm's length lay Fargo's Colt. She sliced a few times, then glanced around and saw Harmony. "Did our guest appreciate the water or did he want a stronger drink?"

Fargo stepped into the open, giving Harmony a push. "The water was fine, ma'am. I thank you for your kindness, but I really must be going."

Maude showed no fear whatsoever. She placed the knife down and stepped back, her hands out from her sides. "Do as you want. All I ask is that you don't hurt my girls."

"I never intended to hurt any of you," Fargo said. "It's a pity you wouldn't believe me." He walked to the table so he could holster the Colt. As he raised his face to the women, he noticed both of them looking past him. Maude showed shock, Harmony was smirking. He shifted, but too slowly. It felt as if an invisible hammer clipped him on the shoulder, causing him to stagger against the table. He thought Leland had attacked him. Then he saw Sym.

Her hair and clothes were dusty, her face glistened with sweat. Rage distorted her features as she swung a long metal bar a second time.

Fargo leaped to the right and heard the bar whiz past him. He'd meant his claim about not wanting to hurt them, but he had to dispose of the big woman before her sister or mother lent a hand. Stepping in close as Sym drew back the bar, he rammed the rifle stock into her abdomen. Sputtering, Sym doubled over, putting her temple in easy reach. A single tap of the barrel was enough to flatten her.

"You scum!" Harmony cried, lunging.

Fargo whirled, the rifle tucked to his hip, halting her charge. To their mother, he said, "I'm sorry. Sym is a hellion. I couldn't go easy on her."

Maude made no comment.

"Since I don't want your husband to get any harebrained ideas, I'd like Harmony to ride out of the gorge with me," Fargo suggested.

"I'd rather die!" the blonde said.

Maude put a hand on her daughter's shoulder. "Go with the man, girl. I don't think he'll hurt you none."

"Ma, no! You saw what he just did."

"He could just as easily have killed Sym. I'm commencing to think we've misjudged him." Maude folded her hands in front of her. "Mister, you will let her go once you're in the clear?"

"You have my word," Fargo said.

Harmony folded her arms across her chest. "Your word isn't worth a pile of bear squat, as far as I'm concerned. I'm not going anywhere with you, and that's final."

"Wrong." Fargo didn't care to stand there arguing when Leland Britches might spot him at any second and open fire. His patience at an end, he grabbed Harmony's wrist and roughly hauled her toward the entrance. She kicked him in the shin, then tried to tear loose.

"Harmony, you do as I told you, you hear?" Maude scolded.

From then on Harmony gave Fargo no trouble. The horses were right where Sym had left them. He discarded the rifle, drew his pistol, and set off down the gulch at a lope. Harmony rode beside him, her long hair flying. They went halfway before Fargo spied Leland Britches, who was in the creek panning for color. Leland gawked but made no move for his rifle, propped on a handy boulder.

Fargo was as glad as could be when they had put Grizzly Gulch behind them and they were riding southward through the forest. At a small clearing he reined up, but only long enough to tell Harmony she could go home. He hadn't uttered a word, however, when the brush crackled and from out of the surrounding pines rode four men.

It was Rand and Brickman with two others. And all four had their revolvers out.

5

On seeing the timbermen, Skye Fargo dropped his hand to his Colt. He would get one or two before they got him, and his only regret was that Abe Decker wasn't with them. But in the split second before Fargo drew he saw that Rand and Brickman were grinning broadly and none of the four had their six-shooters pointed at him. They were acting as if he was a long-lost friend, not an enemy.

"Good job, Dunn!" Brickman said.

"The boss will be happy to get his hands on that one," Rand remarked.

Harmony Britches slashed her reins at Fargo's face, missing by an inch. "You son of a bitch! You were lying through your teeth the whole time! I knew it! I hope Sym skins you alive for this!"

Fargo just sat there. Both sides were doing it again. They still assumed he was Dunn even though by now one or the other faction should have realized the truth. It was too ridiculous for words. He didn't know whether he should laugh at their stupidity or beat his head against a tree in frustration. Since their mistake had spared him from a gunfight he decided to play along awhile longer yet. "What are you doing here?" he asked Decker's men.

Rand answered. "Abe sent us to keep an eye on Grizzly Gulch. He had a hunch you'd show up around here sooner or later."

"Yep." Brickman had to contribute his two-bits worth. "He figured you'd chase the bushwhacker clear back here." His flat eyes fixed on Harmony. "Is she the one?"

Before Fargo could reply, the blonde let loose with a string of oaths and finished with, "I did it and I'm glad I tried! I only wish I'd killed you two jackasses."

A burly timberman nudged his horse next to hers so he could stroke her shiny hair. "She sure is a pretty hellcat. What say we tear those buckskins off and treat ourselves before taking her back? Decker will never find out."

Fargo wasn't about to let any harm come to Harmony. He knocked the man's hand off her head and declared, "I'm the one who caught her. I'm the one who will say how she's to be treated. And I say no one lays a finger on her."

The burly henchman had his pistol in his right hand. He started to lift it but stopped when Rand barked his name.

"Terrell! That's enough out of you. Dunn is right. The boss wants the Britches clan dead, but he's made it plain he doesn't want any of the women abused. The man who does will answer to him." Rand paused. "And you're really not fool enough to think you'd stand a prayer, are you?"

"No one can be as tough as you keep making him out to be," Terrell said.

"You haven't been with us that long or you'd know differently," Rand said. "Abe could lick you with one arm and not work up a sweat. You don't want to make him mad."

Terrell chuckled, but he moved his horse away from Harmony's. "I ain't scared of him or any other man. He's paying my wages, though, so I ought to do as he wants."

Fargo was the only one who observed Brickman and Rand share a sly glance. He wondered why as Brickman grasped Harmony's reins and the timbermen trotted westward toward the Rogue River. Falling in behind them, he tried to give Harmony a reassuring smile when she turned his way. Her bitter look said more than words; she wanted him dead in the worst way.

The ride was uneventful. None of the timbermen were talkative so Fargo was left alone. At a well-marked crossing they waded their mounts through waist-high water. From there a rutted dirt road wound upward into high hills. They had not gone far when the forest echoed to strident cries and the crash of downed trees. A timber crew was hard at work harvesting an adjacent slope. Fargo saw two men handling a saw twice as long as the Ovaro, cutting into a pine with smooth, practiced strokes. Atop another tree another man was sawing off the top. Elsewhere felled trees were being trimmed and loaded into a huge wagon.

"More of Decker's outfit?" Fargo asked.

"He has three crews out at all times," Rand revealed. "Those settlers up in the Willamette Valley need all the good lumber they can get their hands on. Houses and barns and the like are sprouting up all over. Plus we sell some to a few mining operations."

The news further perplexed Fargo. With the lumber market booming and only going to get better as more and more pilgrims flocked to the Oregon Territory, Decker stood to be a rich man eventually. Why, then, was Decker interested in Grizzly Gulch? From what Fargo had seen, Leland Britches was barely able to support his family on the gold found there. Did Decker know something Leland didn't? Was there a rich vein Leland had yet to discover?

Soon the road curled over a hill into a green valley. To the south stood a sawmill bustling with activity. A large sign, erected over a fork in the road that led to the mill, proclaimed: THE RED DOG MILL. ABRAHAM DECKER, OWNER. Underneath, a smaller sign read: LUMBER, $40 A THOUSAND.

Across from the sign another fork circled around to the front of a palatial home but half completed. Workmen were erecting a wall while others sanded a column that would grace a wide portico. No expense was being spared in the construction and it showed.

Fargo reined up beside Harmony. She wouldn't so much as glance at him and edged her horse away. He heard Brickman snicker.

"You must not be the hellcat's type, Dunn. Get too close and she might try to scratch your eyes out."

The front door opened and out walked Decker, talking to a man in dirty overalls who carried a T square. Decker saw them and shooed the man off with a wave of his hand. "Well, well," he siad, stepping to Harmony's mount and resting a hand on the bridle. "Look what the cat drug in. And here I thought you swore that you'd never set foot on my property again. How are you, Harmony?"

"Go to hell."

"Is that any way to talk to an old friend?" Decker asked in mock dismay.

"We were never close," Harmony said, giving him the same sort of look she had given Fargo previously. "And we never will be, not after what you've done."

In the blink of an eye Decker became so incensed he reached up and yanked her off the horse. Looking like an enraged bull about to charge, he shoved her and snorted, "You're a fine one to be criticizing me! The Britches family aren't the saints they'd have most folks believe. You're conniving snakes in the grass, every last one of you."

Harmony pulled his hands loose from her shirt. "And what are you? What do you call a man who hires a notorious back shooter to wipe out an entire family?"

For a moment Fargo thought Decker would strike her. The lumberman's brawny hands clenched and his powerful body shook as if in the grip of the ague.

"I never hired Mr. Dunn. He's an old acquaintance, is all, and he happened to be in the area."

The barefaced lie had to be for the benefit of the listening workers, Fargo realized. Only a handful of Decker's men must know about his grudge, and probably even fewer about his plan to slay all the Britches. Decker suddenly motioned at him, so Fargo dismounted and walked with the timber king to a completed corner of the house where there were no workmen.

"Why the hell did you bring her here? Are you out of your mind? I can't be seen anywhere near any of the Britches until this whole thing is done with."

"Rand and Brickman brought her," Fargo said. "I just tagged along."

"Those idiots," Decker growled. "Between the two of them, they don't have enough brains to fill a thimble. But I expect better from you, Dunn. You came highly recommended as a man who knows how to handle these situations."

"Now hold on," Fargo said, playing his part. "You can't blame me. I still don't know what the situation is. Our little chat was interrupted, remember?"

Decker puffed his cheeks but didn't argue. Tramping to the horses, he smiled at Harmony and announced loudly enough for the men down at the sawmill to hear, "I'm sorry for any inconvenience you were caused. You're free to go if you'd like."

Rand was more flustered than the blonde. "What?" he exclaimed. "But, boss, she's the one who tried to blow your head off. Ain't you going to do something about that?"

Abe Decker wore a pained expression when he turned to his top man. "Has she admitted taking shots at us?"

"Yes, sir," Rand said. "And me and the boys heard her. You could have her arrested and we'd testify for you."

"Yes, have me arrested," Harmony said. "Drag me all the way to Salem or even Portland. The law there might be interested to learn that Vic Dunn is in this neck of the woods."

Fargo saw Decker hesitate and assumed Decker was actually considering the idea. It was reckless of Harmony to goad them since it was doubtful she'd survive the journey. Decker wouldn't let her talk to anyone wearing a badge. "The woman is lying," he stated. "She wasn't the one who shot at us. Her sister did the honors."

"You miserable son of a bitch!" Harmony said. "Who asked you to butt in?"

Decker acted relieved. "Which one of your sisters was it?" he inquired.

"Tune," Harmony said shrewishly.

"Liar. Your father doesn't let her handle a gun yet," Decker said. "I'd guess it was Sym. She's man enough to pull off an ambush in broad daylight."

Rand and Brickman laughed at the joke. Even Fargo grinned, while stepping to the Ovaro to be close to his Sharps. He would fight to have Harmony set free if Decker chose not to. But his worry was needless.

"Ride on home, hussy. Tell your father that this isn't settled yet, not by a long shot. And tell him that next time he shouldn't send a woman to do a job he ought to do himself," Decker said.

"You leave Pa out of this, damn you," Harmony said. "He's not the one and you know it."

"No, I didn't, until now," Decker said.

Fargo had no idea what they were talking about. Nor did he understand why Harmony lost her head and picked that moment to haul off and kick the timberman in the groin. Decker let out a strangled cry and doubled over as Harmony pivoted and sprang to her mount. Jumping into the saddle, she turned her horse directly into those of the men who had brought her. Their horses shied, creating an opening through which she bolted like a jackrabbit. Several of Decker's men raised their pistols but held their fire when Decker bellowed for them not to shoot. All, that is, save one.

The lumberjack named Terrell banged off a hasty shot. At the blast Harmony slumped forward. She was in the clear and neither slowed nor stopped, dashing at a brash gallop toward the road. The men were so busy trying to control their spooked mounts that none thought to give chase.

But Fargo did. He suspected that Harmony's horse was fleeing of its own accord. Swinging onto the Ovaro, he raced off.

"Dunn! Come back here!" Decker bawled.

Fargo wasn't about to. He cut directly to the road, gaining yards on Harmony. Her horse had its tail arched and wasn't about to stop for anything short of Grizzly Gulch or death. It skirted a wagon lumbering toward the sawmill and in doing so passed under a low limb that nearly took Harmony's head off.

Fargo pushed the stallion to its limits, anxious to overtake the woman before tragedy struck. He was climbing the hill leading out of the small valley when a dust cloud a quarter of a mile behind him revealed Decker's men and possibly Decker himself were coming on fast.

Using his spurs, Fargo gradually caught up with Harmony. He saw her eyes were closed, and that if not for her shirt catching on her saddle horn she would have fallen off long ago. Reining the Ovaro nearer, he leaned and forked an arm around Harmony's narrow waist. He tugged but nothing happened. Her shirt was snagged fast and one foot wedged in a stirrup.

Fargo clawed at the shirt, trying to loosen it. The tough buckskin refused to budge. Bending lower, he pulled on her leg until the boot shook loose. She sagged in the opposite direction and almost slipped off, forcing him to partially leave the saddle to retain his grip. Again he worked at the shirt, sliding it back and forth. Her weight handicapped him or he would have had it off in a second. Persisting, he gripped the buckskin with all his might, then heaved.

Harmony slipped free so swiftly that Fargo was thrown backward by the strength of his own pull. Frantically he clutched at his own saddle horn with his other hand and kept himself from toppling. Her horse galloped on down the road, but Fargo didn't. He cut into the trees on his right, went a dozen yards, and halted under the full limbs of a pine. Hooves drummed to the west as he draped the woman across his thighs.

Abe Decker and his men were so intent on catching Fargo and Harmony that not a single one looked to either side of the road. Grim as death, they sped around the next bend.

Fargo figured they wouldn't catch Harmony's horse before it reached the Rogue River. By then he would be miles off, and since none of the timber crowd could track a bull buffalo through a mud wallow, he had succeeded in giving them the slip.

Riding southward, Fargo sought a creek. He had to go over five miles, but at length he stopped in a clearing rimmed by briars. Easing from the saddle, he lifted Harmony off and set her on her back. The wound was shallow, no more than a crease on the side of her forehead, enough to render her unconscious but not do serious harm.

From his saddlebags Fargo took a cloth he used for cleaning his guns. He dipped it in the creek and wrung it out several times to clean it, then folded it in half and pressed the soft material to Harmony's brow. Next he made a fire and soon had a pot of coffee boiling.

Harmony Britches groaned and tossed awhile before her eyes opened. She saw him and scrambled to a sitting posture. The compress fell off, brushing her eyelids and startling her. She clutched it, stared at it a moment, then at him. "What's this? Where am I? What's going on?"

"I got you away from Decker."

"Why would you do that for me?"

"You figure it out," Fargo said, checking to see if the coffee was done. He was tired of trying to explain himself to thickheaded people who already had him pegged as someone else. Filling his cup, he offered it to her. "Here. This might clear some of the cobwebs. You were grazed by a bullet."

Harmony gingerly felt along her temple, then accepted the coffee. "You doctored me?"

"The best I could with what I had at hand," Fargo said. He drank a few swallows straight from the pot, then smacked his lips. Things were looking up for a change. The sun wouldn't set for three hours, giving him plenty of time to drop the blonde off at the gulch and be on his way to California before nightfall.

Harmony had yet to take a sip. She stared at him as if he were a strange creature from some remote land. "Mister, you have me so damned confused, my head hurts."

"It's the wound. Slugs have been known to make quite a dent, even on hard noggins like yours." Fargo stood and walked to the stallion, which hungrily chomped on the sweet grass. He loosened the cinch to give the pinto a breather but didn't take off the saddle. He never knew if Decker's men might show up after all.

"There are some things I don't understand," Harmony said as he strolled back.

"I thought the Britches knew all there is to know," Fargo couldn't resist saying. He was in no mood to be kind, not after all they had put him through.

Harmony disregarded the sarcasm. "If you're not Dunn, then why did you bother to escape from the pit? We would have let you out after Melody confirmed your story. And why did you knock Sym out like you did?"

"I escaped because I don't like being penned up. It's that simple," Fargo answered. "And as for your sister, she was trying to brain me at the time, remember?" He lifted the pot and swirled the coffee. He had a few choice words he'd like to use, but the sight of her red lips and creamy complexion derailed his train of thought. He swallowed, his eyes fastened on the swell of her bosom.

"Well, yes, as I recollect, she was," Harmony said. "But how can you explain letting Rand and them take me to Decker's place?"

"What was I supposed to do? Start a gunfight with you sitting right there? Maybe have you be hit in the crossfire?"

"You didn't shoot because of *me*?" Harmony said.

"You're learning."

Her face a study in bewilderment, Harmony sat silently for a while, sipping and regarding him intently.

"Don't take all day drinking that," Fargo commented. "I have to get you home soon so I can head south."

"You're leaving?"

"I have no reason to stay."

"But Decker—?" Harmony said.

"Abe Decker is your problem, not mine," Fargo said bluntly. "When I first heard he was gunning for your family, I wanted to help you out. And look how I was treated." He removed his hat to run a hand through his thick hair. "Now all of you can kill yourselves off, for all I care. I know when I'm not wanted."

"Maybe Ma was right about you," Harmony said. She gulped the rest of her coffee, then held out the cup. "Can I have a little more before we go? Please?"

Fargo was impatient to be off but he had never been one to refuse a pretty woman, especially one who asked so nicely. He poured a second cup and couldn't help but note the manner in which she openly admired him while he did. Her knuckles brushed the back of his hand as she lowered her arm, tingling his skin. When she leaned back, her breasts seemed to heave against her buckskin shirt as if trying to burst free.

Harmony drank only a tiny bit, cleared her throat, and said, "Looking back, I can see where we might have misjudged you. Lord knows, you've had more than enough chances to kill us if that was your aim." She gently placed her hand on his. "I only pray you'll believe me when I tell you how sorry I am. And I'd stake my life that the rest of my family will feel the same."

"Apology accepted," Fargo said. The warmth of her palm made him think of warmer parts of her anatomy, and he shook his head to dispel the notion. He still had no intention of staying in the Rogue River region past nightfall.

"What do you do for a living, Mr. Fargo?" Harmony asked sweetly, sliding nearer.

"Scout, track, trailblaze, whatever comes along."

60

"Are you very handy with that shooting iron?"

"Handier than most," Fargo said, without being boastful. He'd had to be in order to survive as long as he had. Wilderness life wasn't for amateurs and greenhorns.

"Are you just as good with that big old Sharps I see on your horse?"

"Better," Fargo said, wondering why she was suddenly so interested in his marksmanship. One minute she'd been as cold as well water toward him, the next as friendly as a saloon dove. Women were like that, though. Fire and ice wrapped in attractive packages, as unpredictable as grizzlies and sometimes twice as dangerous.

"It was awfully nice of you to want to side with us in our dispute with Abe," Harmony said, sidling even closer. "Awfully nice."

"I have this bad habit of sticking my nose where it doesn't belong," Fargo said. "One of these days I'd better outgrow it or it's liable to be the death of me."

Harmony smiled. "I'd hate to see you come to any harm after all the grief we've put you through." She draped her hand on his forearm. "You must think we're terrible beasts, the way we've been acting."

"I've met friendlier people," Fargo said.

"Don't hold it against us, handsome," Harmony said. "Our family has been under a big strain lately, what with Decker wanting us dead and him sending for that horrible Vic Dunn and all."

"It's understandable," Fargo sympathized, and was rewarded with an affectionate pat on the shoulder. Her fingernails lightly scraped his ear.

"Won't Abe be mad when he learns he's been tricked!" Harmony declared. "Why, he'll want your hide too. I wouldn't be surprised if he sends Dunn after you as well as us."

The thought was troubling, and one Fargo hadn't considered. Decker might think he knew too much for his own good and had to be eliminated. He leaned back to reflect on the matter but wasn't afforded the opportunity.

"Seems to me I ought to thank you properlike for all you've

done for me," Harmony announced, pressing flush against him and poising her lips next to his. "That is, if you don't have any objections?"

Their mouths met.

6

Skye Fargo had been kissed by more women in his lifetime than most ten men put together. From the Mississippi to the Pacific, from Canada to Mexico, he had made love to some of the most beautiful females alive. Few kissed as divinely as Harmony Britches. Her lips were as soft as a feather, as smooth as silk. And she knew just how to use them.

Harmony's warm breath fanned Fargo's cheek as she ground herself into him, her full mounds rubbing his chest through their buckskin shirts. Her hands drifted over his ribs and back, one dallying above his belt.

Fargo darted his tongue between her hot lips. Her moist tongue met his and entwined. She tasted like cedar, as if she had chewed bits of pine bark to freshen her breath. Her hair smelled equally fragrant, tantalizing Fargo with its heady aroma. He ran a hand down her spine and felt her arch her back.

"Ummmmm, yes," Harmony husked. "I knew you'd be worth it."

Worth what? Fargo would have asked had his mouth not been occupied. Lying flat on his side, he cupped her buttocks and mashed her hips into his groin. Her breath grew hotter and she thrust into him as if trying to impale herself on his pole through his pants.

"I want you," Harmony said.

Fargo could see that for himself but he was not about to rush. Too many days had gone by since he'd last enjoyed the feel of a voluptuous body next to his. He kissed her cheeks, her chin, her neck. Harmony squirmed and cooed. Kneading her thighs, he lathered her throat from ear to ear and then fastened his lips on an earlobe. She panted heavily, her left leg inserting itself between his legs and rubbing up and down.

His manhood surging, Fargo pushed his loins hard against her nether mound, causing her to wriggle more deliciously than before. She raked his shoulders with her nails while nibbling on his face.

"You sure know how to make a lady feel all weak inside," Harmony whispered.

Fargo smothered her mouth with his and tugged at the bottom of her shirt, hiking the buckskin high enough to expose her glorious globes. She wore no undergarments. Bending, he encircled a rigid nipple with his lips and worked the nipple around and around. Harmony hissed happily, then boldly reached down to cup his pole.

Exquisite sensations shot through Fargo's body. He switched to her other breast, massaging it with his hand and his mouth, relishing the way her hips swayed in rhythm to his movements. She knew how to give pleasure as well as receive it, and she wasn't one of those women who liked to lie as limp as a rag while the man did all the work.

Fargo grasped the top of her pants and shoved. They caught around her hips. Looking down, he saw a cord she used as a crude belt. He unfastened the knot and the pants came off easily, revealing a pair of legs that would have been the envy of every dance hall girl alive. And unlike the pale legs of saloon women, Harmony's were bronzed brown by the sun and rippling with muscle. Country girls were as healthy as thoroughbreds in that regard, and twice as spirited.

Harmony couldn't get enough of him. She explored every nook and cranny, rubbing him everywhere she could reach. After a while she made bold to slip a hand under the top of his pants and stroked him lightly.

Fargo was doing some stroking of his own. His finger had found her tunnel. By poking it in and out, over and over, he rapidly aroused Harmony to a fever pitch. She humped her lovely bottom against his hand, trying to suck his finger up inside of her. When he dropped his mouth to her navel, she groaned, and she kept on groaning as he kissed a path to the junction of her thighs.

"What do you have in mind, lover?"

Spreading her legs wide, Fargo knelt and replaced his finger with his tongue. She tasted like nectar, and he couldn't get enough of her. Like a man half starved, he licked her core, holding on tight as she bucked and heaved and went into a delirium of ecstasy.

Fargo played her like a master musician would play a violin. Time and again he brought her to the brink of sexual rapture, only to let her coast down again so he could start over. By the time he was ready to enter her, she was slick with sweat and quivering with desire.

Unhitching his gunbelt and his britches, Fargo slowly fed his sword into her hot sheath. Her walls closed on him like velvet gloves, trembling uncontrollably. He held still a full minute to build her anticipation, then he pounded into her with a vengeance.

"Ohhhhhhh!" Harmony moaned.

Fargo adopted a regular cadence, rocking on his knees and palms, burying himself to the hilt each time. Harmony met his ardor with unbridled passion, her teeth digging into his shoulder, her nails lacerating his back. She wrapped her legs around his waist to give him better leverage.

It was all Fargo could do not to explode prematurely. She was all any man could want in a woman, and so much more. Her nipples rubbed his chest, her thighs molded to his. When they kissed again her mouth was molten fire. He continued ramming into her, his whole body racked by bolts of sensual delight. Harmony suddenly threw back her head, her lips curling back over her white teeth, and let out a screech. Her delectable bottom worked in a frenzy, lifting his into the air.

Then Fargo spurted. A sensational spasm shot from the bottom of his toes to the base of his skull. He stroked and stroked until he was utterly spent and collapsed on top of her. He could feel her heart beating wildly, matching his own.

Harmony lay still until she caught her breath. Twisting, she grinned and said, "If I'd had any notion what I was missing, I would have jumped you long ago."

Fargo slid off her, onto his back, and cradled his head in his hand. She nuzzled him, then lay with her head on his shoulder. The sun had dipped halfway to the horizon. A few low clouds, shaped like fluffy pillows, sailed eastward on the stiff breeze, which cooled Fargo's body and brought goose bumps to his legs.

"That was nice," Harmony said, looking at him as if waiting for an answer.

"Yes, it was," Fargo allowed. He felt sleepy but wouldn't allow himself to doze off.

"We should do it again real soon."

Fargo glanced at her. "I'm heading for California this evening, remember?"

"Shucks, you can't travel at night. It's too dangerous. Stick around until morning. You're welcome to stay at the gulch, if you'd like."

"I'm moving on," Fargo insisted. "There will be a full moon tonight. By morning I'll be almost to the border."

"You'd leave, after what we just did?" Harmony sounded affronted. She propped herself on an elbow and asked in a hurt tone, "Don't I mean any more to you than that? What kind of man are you that you can take advantage of a woman and then ride off without a second thought?"

The accusation was the kind Fargo would expect from a prim schoolmarm, not a wild, carefree woman like Harmony. And since she had practically thrown herself at him, he thought it hypocritical of her to blame him for doing what came naturally. "I didn't make any promises," he pointed out.

"Well, I never!" Harmony said, sitting up. "If you ask me, you're not much of a gentleman."

"I haven't claimed to be," Fargo said lazily. He began to suspect she had a hidden motive for making love to him, and her next statement confirmed it.

"Most men would be too grateful to go riding off and leave an innocent family in peril. Most men would stick around awhile to help out."

"I'm not like most men," Fargo said, which was true in one respect. Most were content to marry their sweethearts and settle down to raise a pack of kids. He had never had such an urge and likely never would. Wanderlust had claimed him at an early age, giving him a passion for travel few men possessed. He always had to see what lay over the next ridge or the next mountain. Roaming free was as much a part of him as breathing.

Agitated, Harmony dressed quickly. "You might as well take me home, then. I wouldn't want to delay your precious journey to California."

Fargo would have been content to lie there for a few more minutes. Sighing, he stood, adjusted his clothes, and strapped on the Colt. The coffeepot he upended and stuffed in a saddle-bag.

"You'll at least have a meal with my family before you go?"

"And be shot by Sym or your father? No thanks." Fargo cinched up the Ovaro, climbed into the creaking saddle, and held his hand down. "Climb aboard."

Harmony hesitated, pouting. She stamped her foot once as might a petulant child, gripped his arm, and swung up behind him. Instead of wrapping her arms around his waist, she gripped the fringe on his shoulders so she wouldn't have to touch him. "I'm set."

Fargo grinned and headed out, bearing eastward at a lope toward the Rogue River. He figured that by now Decker had caught the riderless horse and was in a black mood. Decker would be wondering why the two of them had disappeared and might begin to guess the truth. Fargo knew he'd do well to avoid the timberman on his way out of the territory.

There was another factor to consider, one that might work in the Britches' favor. Evidently Decker had been trying to keep his hiring of Vic Dunn as much of a secret as he could to prevent stories from being spread which might eventually be overheard by lawmen. But now the workers at the house had heard Harmony's accusation and seen her shot by Terrell. Within a week everyone within a hundred miles would know Decker was out to eliminate the Britches. Fargo hoped the man had the good sense to call off the feud before it went any further.

Staying well clear of the road, Fargo reached the gently flowing river an hour before sundown. The crossing was to the north, around a bend. Thinking that Decker might have posted men to keep a lookout, Fargo entered the water right there. The river rose to the pinto's knees, then to its belly. Without warning it stumbled, recovered, and pulled at its front legs. Fargo leaned forward and realized it was bogged in deep mud.

He cut to the right and used his spurs harder than he normally would. The stallion gave a powerful wrench and tore loose. Harmony flung her arms around Fargo so she wouldn't fall.

Picking his way with the utmost care, Fargo avoided the muddy sections. A few large Chinook salmon glided gracefully off at the pinto's approach. It was said the Rogue was a fisherman's paradise. Had time permitted, Fargo would have tried his hand at catching a few.

A cleft in the opposite bank gave them the means of reaching the top, and from there Fargo rode cross-country through heavy woodland. Moss covered many of the trees. Ferns grew in abundance. Several times he saw deer, and once a large bull elk trotted into the brush to his right.

They were a mile from Grizzly Gulch when Harmony broke her silence. "Have you changed your mind about staying awhile?"

"No," Fargo said.

"Men!" Harmony muttered, once again taking hold of the fringe. "You're all as contrary as mules." She held her tongue for about ten seconds. "What harm could it do you to stick around? I thought you were interested in helping us fight Decker?"

"I was."

"What changed your mind? Being thrown in the pit?"

"That was part of it," Fargo said. "Mainly I'm not willing to get involved since you're not willing to tell me the reason Decker wants your family dead."

"Who says I'm not? He's after our gold."

"It won't wash, Harmony," Fargo told her. "I doubt your father has found much. And I heard the talk you had with Decker at his house. There's more to this than either of you are letting on."

Harmony had no reply to make. She dropped her hands to her lap and sulked the rest of the way.

Slowing as he neared their destination, Fargo cautiously avoided open spaces. Decker had sent men to watch the gulch once; he might have done so again. When assured it was safe, Fargo rode to the entrance and offered his hand to Harmony. "Here. I'll help you."

"I can manage by my lonesome," she said coldly. Hopping

down, she gave him a dirty look, then stomped off. "And if I never see you again, it'll be too soon."

"Give my regards to your mother," Fargo said, which made her madder. She swiveled and seemed about to give him a tongue-lashing, but with a toss of her head she resumed tramping into the gulch.

"Women," Fargo said to the stallion, and turned southward at long last. He knew it would be wise to stay clear of the established trails until he was well beyond Decker's reach, so for the next two hours he pushed on through verdant woodland. Soon twilight shrouded the country in gloom that was presently relieved by the rising of the moon.

Fargo took a piece of jerky from his saddlebags and munched on the salty meat while riding, enjoying the serenity. Prior to sunset the forest had rung to the noisy chirps of birds and the excited chattering of squirrels. Now it was quiet, restful.

By rights Fargo shouldn't have a care in the world. But he did. Try as he might not to, he kept thinking about the Britches and the fate they were certain to suffer if Decker won. He told himself again and again that it was none of his business but his conscience would not stop pricking him.

At length Fargo turned westward to locate the main trail. From a low hill he spied a pale ribbon of trampled earth that stood out in stark contrast to the dark green of the surrounding forest. He was descending to it when he spotted another rider coming along the trail from the direction of California. At first he thought nothing of it. Then he noticed the man's horse had white splotches.

Fargo reined up twenty feet from the trail in a cluster of madrones. He felt a little foolish hiding but something told him that he should. He heard hoofbeats, the clomp of the hooves growing louder and louder. Around a turn came the rider, a big man astride a fine calico mare. The man favored a fancy Mexican saddle adorned with silver. Like Fargo, he wore buckskins, but he had a black hat, not white. His features were hard to see in the dark but there was no mistaking the cruel cast to them. He had a beard, clipped short. In a holster on either hip rested a pearl-handled pistol.

It had to be Vic Dunn, the paid killer. Fargo was certain. He was surprised when Dunn abruptly reined up and glanced sharply toward the madrones. The man couldn't have heard anything; he must have the senses of a mountain lion.

Fargo held himself still, his hand on his Colt. A small voice at the back of his head urged him to pull his six-gun and shoot the rider dead, but he had never resorted to a cowardly ambush and wasn't about to now. The man stared a short while, then rode on, looking back every so often. In time he was lost around another bend.

Moving to the trail, Fargo swung the pinto southward. He broke into a trot, eager to make up for lost time. The image of Dunn kept popping into his mind no matter how many times he shrugged it off. Fargo had met his share of dangerous men in his travels and he could tell that Dunn was one of the deadliest. The way the man carried himself, the way he moved, his animal senses, all were earmarks of a born killer. The Britches didn't stand a prayer.

Fargo told himself he didn't care. They had beaten him, tried to shoot him, thrown him into a hole in the ground. Worse, they had a secret they were hiding, something that had to do with Abe Decker and his hatred of them. He didn't feel he could trust them completely and he had to be able to rely on them if he was going to put his life at risk on their behalf.

He rode for miles. In the distance Mount Shasta reared into the starry sky like an earthen colossus, its summit crowned in a mantle of snow that gleamed a pale white in the moonlight. By tomorrow night Mt. Shasta would be behind him, and so would the Britches.

It must have been nine o'clock when Fargo drew rein on a ridge and turned in the saddle to survey the stretch of Oregon Territory he had covered. Somewhere back there the Britches were asleep in the remote grotto they called a home. Somewhere back there Abe Decker was probably filling Vic Dunn in on the job he wanted done. Come morning, Dunn would go about earning his pay. By nightfall it would be all over.

Fargo raised the reins, then suddenly wheeled the stallion and galloped northward, back over the trail he had just traveled. "Damn," he said to himself, and repeated it a dozen yards later, only louder. "Damn!" He was a fool for getting involved, a fool for trying to help a family that was just as likely

70

to shoot him on sight as they were the man out to kill them. And fools seldom lasted long on the frontier.

The Ovaro had been on the go so long that it started to flag shortly before midnight. Fargo decided to rest until morning rather than ride into Grizzly Gulch in the middle of the night and be blasted before he could explain himself. In a clearing by the Rogue River he made a cold camp, filling his belly with enough jerky to hold him until he could enjoy a proper meal.

Fargo lay awake for the longest while, marveling at his knack for getting into trouble. Next to attracting pretty women like honey attracted bears, it was one of his main talents. No matter where he went, he always ran into someone in need, someone being bullied or abused, someone who needed a protector. And nine times out of ten he'd volunteer for the job without being asked. It made him wonder if deep down he wasn't a glutton for punishment.

The squawks of playful jays awakened Fargo before sunrise. He tucked in his clothes, threw his saddle on the Ovaro, pulled the picket pin, and rode on as the golden rim of the sun peeked above the eastern mountains.

Fargo had no idea whether Vic Dunn was stalking the Britches already or not. Taking nothing for granted, he made a circuit of the tract of trees fronting the gulch before he ventured to ride into the opening.

Right away Fargo knew something was wrong. It was too quiet, even for that time of the morning. Birds should be singing and small animals should be out. But there were none. Not so much as an insect disturbed the silence of Grizzly Gulch.

Fargo yanked his Sharps loose, braced the stock on his thigh, and rode deeper into the shadows cast by the high walls, his thumb on the hammer. The mining equipment was where he had seen it last. He stood in the stirrups for a better look at the trees bordering the grotto but saw no movement. Nor was there any smoke to show the stove was being used.

There were scores of tracks, though. Since Fargo had left, a large group of riders had come and gone. He could guess who, and why.

Hurrying to the trees, Fargo dismounted and worked near enough to see under the overhang. The furniture was where it should be but not a single Britches was at home, not even Melody, who had been sick with fever and too weak to go anywhere. Going in, Fargo hunted for clues and found multiple scoff marks left by a lot of boots.

Now what should he do? Fargo asked himself. He couldn't go riding over to Decker's since in all likelihood the real Vic Dunn had already paid the lumberman a visit and Decker was gunning for him. Yet he could think of nowhere else to look. Mounting, he rode from the gulch and took the same trail Rand and Brickman had taken the day before.

Fargo hadn't gone far when he came to where the most recent sets of tracks bore to the east rather than to the west, as they should. It puzzled him. He mulled over whether to go on to Decker's or to follow the new trail and picked Decker's.

It seemed to Fargo that every time he turned around he was crossing the Rogue. He used the crossing and took the road on the fly. Before reaching the little valley in which the sawmill was nestled, he passed a rumbling wagon laden with freshly sawn wood. The two men on the seat hardly gave him a glance.

Fargo left the road well before coming in sight of the mill and house. He rode in a half circle so he could approach the house from the rear. From the concealment of a stand of pines he saw the workers framing a wall but no sign of Abe Decker or the rough crowd who usually rode with them.

Keeping hidden, Fargo rode around to check the mill. Logs were being unloaded out back and several men were operating the blade, but again Abe Decker wasn't there.

Fargo figured he had made a mistake. Decker wouldn't bring the Britches to his home for the workers to see. Frowning at his oversight, blaming it on fatigue, he made for the river, intending to find the trail that led eastward and follow it until he came on the timber king or the bodies. As he gained the road he saw another wagon directly ahead. The driver had it positioned smack in the middle, leaving little space on either side for anyone to go around. Fargo cupped a hand to his mouth and shouted, "Hey! Move to one side or the other! You're blocking the road." The wagon slowly moved to the right so he reined to the left to go around and received a shock that drew him up short.

Galloping toward him were Decker and five others including Rand and Brickman. At sight of him Decker gave a yell and they came on faster.

7

Skye Fargo had every reason to expect to be shot on sight, but not one of Decker's men made a move to draw a gun. He wondered where the hired killer had gotten to, and if the Britches were already dead and buried. Then he received a second surprise.

"Dunn!" Decker snapped, reining up. "What the hell is the matter with you? Where did you get to this time? I thought you went after Harmony. Where is she?"

Fargo couldn't believe his luck. They still mistook him for the killer. Yet it raised a crucial question: Why hadn't the real Dunn contacted Decker?

"I'm waiting for an answer," the timberman said testily. "We caught her horse, but by then there was no sign of her, or of you. What happened?"

Fargo couldn't very well admit his deception. "I took care of her," he said, which was true as far as it went.

Decker smiled, the tension draining from him. "Is that so? Well, it's about time something went my way. Nice work. Now all you have to do is deal with the rest and you'll get your money."

"You haven't told me yet why you want them dead," Fargo said.

"And I'm not about to. Let's just say that they've crossed me one time too many and I won't be satisfied until each and every one of them is three feet under."

"Even the mother and the little girl?"

Decker was a man of mercuric moods. He bristled and clenched a fist as if to strike, but changed his mind. "Since when did the famous Vic Dunn get so righteous? I'd heard that you would kill anyone for money, even your own mother. So

74

what difference does it make if Maude and Tune are on my list? Do what you have to and quit pestering me with questions." With that, Decker lashed his bay and rode on around, his men dutifully following.

Fargo rode to the crossing. He had to find the Britches, and quickly, but he had no idea where to look. The trail that led eastward from the gulch might be a good place to start. So would the trading post. It was closer, and it was the social hub of the territory, the place to learn the latest news and gossip. Maybe Vereen had heard something.

Fargo had another reason for picking the post first. Vic Dunn might have stopped there, might have given Vereen a clue to where he was headed. Fargo loped along until he crested a knoll and saw smoke spiraling from the post chimney. He also saw a rider approaching.

It was Dunn. The killer slowed and rose in the stirrups, studying Fargo closely. As Dunn came on, he shifted the reins from his right hand to his left and lowered his right hand to his hip, next to his holster. In broad daylight he was even bigger than he had looked on the California trail. In addition to the twin Colts, he had a Bowie knife stuck in his right boot, the hilt exposed so he could bring it into play swiftly.

Fargo slowed. The resemblance Dunn bore to him was uncanny, right down to the color of his eyes. Dunn had one distinguishing feature he didn't, a nasty jagged scar creasing the left cheek. Fargo intended to pass the killer without speaking, but Dunn reined up, so he did the same.

"Howdy, mister," the badman said amiably enough. "Seems to me I've seen you somewhere before."

"Oh?" Fargo said, suspecting that Dunn had spotted him in the madrones the night before.

"Every time I look in a mirror." Dunn's thin lips twisted in an oily grin. "It's spooky, looking at you. Sort of like staring at myself, only you're not as good-looking."

The last thing Fargo had expected Vic Dunn to have was a sense of humor. Most of the professional killers he'd met were somber men, as shut off from life as closed doors.

"Our horses even look alike," Dunn was saying, "but anyone with half a brain would know that my calico isn't quite the same as your high-stepping Ovaro."

At last, someone who knew the difference. "No, they're not," Fargo agreed. He stared at the mare and saw the polished stock of a Sharps exactly like his jutting from the saddle scabbard. "Our rifles are, though."

Dunn glanced at Fargo's scabbard. "The best long guns money can buy," he commented. "Once I picked off a Sioux at eight hundred yards with mine."

"A fine shot," Fargo said, and meant it. Whatever else Dunn might be, he was widely recognized as one of the best marksmen in the country. It was claimed he routinely dropped his victims at ranges of five hundred yards or better. "I've done it a few times myself."

"Do tell." Dunn grinned again, a sinister sort of grin that reminded Fargo of the fierce look of a mad wolf. "Not many men can make the claim. You must be someone I've heard of. Have a name?"

"Sure do," Fargo said, but he didn't reveal it. Better, he felt, to keep Dunn guessing.

Dunn waited a few seconds, then nodded. "Fair enough. I'm not one to pry when a man wants to keep a secret." He tapped the brim of his black hat. "Maybe we'll meet again sometime, mister. Maybe when you least expect. It's a small world, as they say."

Fargo stayed where he was until the killer vanished over the knoll. He couldn't make up his mind whether Dunn had been making small talk or issuing a threat.

All the way to the trading post Fargo's back prickled as if from a rash. He half expected to take a slug but no gunshots rang out. Several times he glanced back but didn't see Dunn. A single horse stood at the hitching post and he tied the stallion beside it, then went in.

Vereen was behind the counter, polishing more glasses. On looking up, he dropped his rag and nearly did the same with a shot glass. "Damn," he blurted. "I thought you'd be halfway to Mexico or Canada by now."

"Why is that?" Fargo responded.

"It would be the smart thing to do after going around pretending you're Vic Dunn." Vereen picked up the rag and waved it at the door. "The real article left not five minutes ago. I don't know what your game is, mister, but it's about time you wised up and headed for parts unknown."

"I aim to stay awhile yet," Fargo said. He slapped a coin on the plank. "How about a whiskey?"

"It's your life," Vereen said. "Though it won't be for much longer once Dunn catches up with you."

"We had a few words on the trail," Fargo said. "He didn't act all that put out with me."

"No?" Vereen plucked a bottle from a shelf. "That's mighty peculiar, since he knows you've been masquerading as him."

"Did you tell him?"

A chair unexpectedly crashed to the floor behind Fargo and a hard-as-nails voice roared out, "No, *I* did, you stinking son of a bitch. Turn around so I can see your face when I blow out your lamp."

Fargo slowly turned, making no sudden moves in case he was already covered, as Vereen moved to one side.

Terrell stood next to one of the tables, an almost empty bottle of rye beside him. In his right hand he clutched his revolver. "That's better," he growled. "I want you to see it coming."

"Did Decker send you?" Fargo asked, stalling, trying to distract the lumberjack so he could go for his Colt.

"Hell, no," Terrell said, taking a step. "Decker fired me! Told me to pack my things and leave before he had me hung from the nearest tree, and all for shooting that uppity bitch, Harmony! He said I didn't know how to listen, that I shouldn't so much as breathe without getting his permission!"

"Then why shoot me if you're no longer working for him?" Fargo asked, easing his right hand off the bar.

"Don't try it!" Terrell thundered, advancing another stride. "I might be drunk, but this close I can still put a bullet into you." He wagged the pistol. "Maybe Decker will have a change of heart when he hears. Maybe he'll hire me back. I'm doing him a favor by killing you."

"Maybe you should ask him first."

Terrell uttered a dry cackle. "Funny man, ain't you? Figured you had everyone hoodwinked, I bet. You had me fooled too, until I rode in here on my way out of the valley. I saw that gent with the scar standing by his paint horse, and I told him that he had a horse just like Vic Dunn's." Terrell came one more step nearer. "He wanted to know what I meant, so I told him. You could have knocked me over with a feather when he told me who he was."

Fargo coiled his leg muscles for the leap. He doubted that he could swat the revolver aside before Terrell fired, but at least he might deflect the gun enough to cause the bullet to miss his vital organs.

"I don't know who you are or what scheme you've hatched, but here's where I put an end to it," Terrell said, steadying his arm. "I think I'll keep that paint of yours. It's better than my own nag."

Fargo glimpsed Vereen out of the corner of an eye, frozen against the back wall. He could expect no help from that quarter. Girding himself, he gripped the edge of the bar for added leverage and planted his toes firmly. Just as he was ready to spring, the front door crashed open and loud laughter filled the room.

Terrell, befuddled by too much rye, did what any other man would do; he glanced at the entrance.

In that moment, Fargo leaped, his left hand batting the revolver as he drove his right fist into Terrell's stomach. The gun went off so near his ear that it sent a lancing pain through his head, and then the two of them toppled into the table, crashing it to the floor along with the bottle. He landed a blow to the jaw that Terrell seemed to hardly feel. Before he could follow through, the lumberjack's heavy boot caught him in the midriff and sent him flying into another table.

Fargo landed on his side. Terrell's gun lay on the floor between them, and he leaped for it at the same time Terrell did to stop Terrell from reaching it. Colliding, they grappled, rolling over and over. Fargo was a big man but his assailant outweighed him by fifty pounds, all of it muscle. As thick fingers closed on Fargo's windpipe, he knew he was in for a hard fight.

Heaving, Fargo tried to throw Terrell off him but the lumberjack clung tenaciously on. Sharp fingernails bit into his flesh as Terrell squeezed.

"You're a dead man, bastard!" Terrell snapped.

Fargo didn't have the breath to argue. He felt as if his neck was slowly being crushed beyond repair, and he had to do something. Putting both palms against Terrell's chin, he shoved, but the man's neck was as thick as a bull's. He rammed a punch to the cheek that split skin and had no other effect. His lungs flared with anguish, as if they were on fire. In desperation he slammed his knee into the bigger man's groin.

That did the trick. Terrell sagged and groaned, spittle rimming his lips, his fingers going slack.

Fargo kneed him again, then pushed. Terrell was flipped to the left, enabling Fargo to rise. He had no sooner stood than the lumberjack was on him, tackling him around the shins. Once more they smashed to the floor. Twisting, Fargo landed a two-punch combination that rocked Terrell but didn't finish him. The man had the constitution of an ox.

Both of them gained their knees at the same time and knelt there slugging it out. Blood pouring from split lips, Terrell battered Fargo with fists as big as hams. Fargo blocked most of the blows but enough slipped his guard to punish him severely. One struck him in the ribs and nearly bowled him over. Fargo immediately straightened, but the moment cost him. Terrell's hand disappeared under his coat and flashed out, holding a glittering Bowie knife.

Nearly taken unawares, Fargo ducked under a slash that would have severed his head from his neck. He grabbed Terrell's wrist and held on. Terrell hit him with the other hand, a stunning jolt to the ear.

The room spun before Fargo's eyes and he could feel himself weakening. The point of the Bowie inched closer to his neck as Terrell, sensing the time was ripe, strained with renewed vigor. It was all Fargo could do to hold the wicked blade at bay.

Suddenly Terrell wrenched his body to the right, flipping Fargo into a chair. Fargo lost his grip and the chair fell on top of him. He threw it at Terrell as the lumberman closed in, and Terrell, as Fargo expected, dodged.

"Let's end this, damn you!" Terrell bellowed, raising the Bowie for a downward slash.

Fargo was ready. He had his hand on the hilt of his Arkansas toothpick, and as Terrell swung, he whipped the throwing knife from his boot and buried it in Terrell's chest just below the sternum. The lumberjack gasped in surprise and tried to fling himself backward but Fargo stabbed him twice more in rapid succession in the same spot.

Whining like an infant, Terrell melted to the floor and lay still, the Bowie dropping from his lifeless fingers.

Fargo slowly stood, using a table for support. He was sore all over and his head throbbed. Just for the hell of it he kicked the Bowie, then walked to the counter. "Where's my whiskey?" he croaked.

Vereen blankly nodded, his gaze on the dead man. He fumbled with the bottle and glass, spilling some. "I saw the whole thing," he said. "It was a clear case of self-defense."

The red-eye seared Fargo's mouth and throat, restoring him. He set the glass down and wiped the toothpick on the proprietor's cloth. "Hope you don't mind."

"Not at all," Vereen said. "Anything you want to do, feel free. Have more whiskey. It's on me."

Fargo downed a second glass in two swallows, then replaced the throwing knife. He tried to think, to plan his next move, but his blood pounded in his temples, making it impossible. The fight had been a close thing, yet it was just the beginning. More blood would have to be shed before the Britches were safe, and some of it might be his own.

"That was sure a sight, mister."

Fargo had forgotten all about the person who had entered at the opportune moment. Young Jess Harper walked to the bar, treading lightly as if afraid to make too much noise.

"I wanted to shoot him for you but I didn't know if you'd be upset with me. Some men like to do their own killing."

Vereen acted annoyed. "Can't you see the man isn't in a talkative frame of mind right now? What are you doing here, anyway?"

"The usual," Jess said, going to a rack that contained a half-dozen large jars. The jars contained horehound candy and other confections. "I can't disappoint my little darling."

The owner snickered and said to Fargo, "He's in love. Or thinks he is. At his age it's all the same thing."

Jess brought back a handful of horehound candy. "Laugh all you want to, Vereen. You're just jealous because you don't have a sweetheart." He deposited the minty sweets. "I'd like these wrapped. With one of them tiny red ribbons, if you don't mind. Tune is real partial to them."

At the mention of one of the Britches, Fargo turned. "Do you know where I can find her family? I need to talk to them."

"No," Jess said, much too quickly. "I don't. I'm buying the candy in case I see her later on." He averted his gaze and nervously tapped his boot while the horehound was wrapped. After paying, he touched his hat and hurried out.

"Not too bright, is he?" Vereen said.

"Who is at that age?" Fargo replied. He pointed at Terrell's body. "Do you need a hand burying him?"

"No, you go on and do what you've got to do. Only—" Vereen hesitated, as if fearful of going on.

"Only what?"

"You are on their side, aren't you? The Britches, I mean? I like them, and I wouldn't want to see any harm come their way." Vereen grinned self-consciously. "I'm sort of partial to one of the daughters, the most beautiful of them all. If she'd have me, I'd marry her in a minute. But she can't be bothered. She thinks I'm not man enough for her."

"Melody and Harmony are eyefuls," Fargo remarked.

"Oh, it's not one of those two. They're too scrawny for my taste. Sym is the one I like. That gal is a mountain of a woman, enough for any ten men."

"True," Fargo said, trying to imagine the portly man and Sym as a couple. Somehow, he couldn't. "And to answer your question, yes, I'd like to help them if they'll let me." He turned on a boot heel and went out before Jess Harper gained too much of a lead.

The young rancher was hundreds of yards to the east, but he wasn't alone. His brother Wesley rode beside him.

That explained the laughter, Fargo reflected as he climbed onto the Ovaro. One brother had gone in while the other waited with the horses. He didn't strike off after them immediately but waited until they were specks the size of ants. It had been obvious Jess Harper lied. The young man did know where the Britches were and was probably taking the candy straight to Tune. Fargo trailed them, always staying far enough back that neither would be apt to notice. Once they reached the forest he closed the gap to within a quarter of a mile. The trees and undergrowth were so thick and there were so many bends to the trail that he was confident they wouldn't see him.

The trail was wide enough to accommodate wagons, deep ruts showing it did regularly. It bore to the northeast after a while, winding along the bottoms of hills and mountains.

Occasionally Fargo heard the brothers laughing. Once, had it not been for Jess's high cackle, he would have blundered into them as they sat letting their horses drink at a stream.

In due course the road came to another small valley lush with grass. Fargo reined up under cover of the pines. A mile away stood a ranch house, stable, and corral. The Harper spread, he supposed. Cattle grazed in scattered clusters everywhere.

Fargo rode to the edge of the trees for a better look. He could see the stretch of road clearly, and for a moment he had the impression something wasn't as it should be. Then he realized the Harper boys weren't anywhere in sight. And hardly had the thought crossed his mind than a rope sailed out of nowhere and settled over his shoulders.

Fargo was torn from the saddle and hit the ground with a thud. He tried to stand but the rope tightened and he was dragged out into the open, wincing when he hit a large rock. By craning his neck he could see Wesley Harper, the rope dallied around Wesley's saddle horn. Suddenly Wesley stopped and Fargo rolled another half-dozen feet. Covered with dust and bits of grass, Fargo pushed to his knees. To his rear there was a metallic click.

"I wouldn't do anything hasty, were I you."

Fargo shifted. Jess Harper had the Navy Colt fixed on him. Evidently the brothers were sharper than he had thought and had noticed him somewhere along the trail.

"I sort of like you, mister," Jess had gone on, "so I don't want to blow a hole in you if you won't give me cause. But I don't like the fact you shadowed us all the way home."

"I need to talk to the Britches," Fargo reiterated. "And I have a feeling you know where to find them."

"Maybe I do, maybe I don't," Jess said. "Whichever, they've made it plain they don't care to talk to you. Maude trusts you, I think, but Leland doesn't. Nor does Sym. She'll tear into you the minute she sets eyes on you."

Fargo slowly slipped the rope off his shoulders. Both brothers had come closer but neither were quite close enough. "So you won't let me see them, even if it's important?"

"No, sir. Sorry," Jess said. "You'd do well to get on your horse and head somewhere else."

"So everyone keeps telling me."

Wesley walked his sorrrel a few feet nearer. "Then why don't you take their advice? Or aren't you smart enough to know when you're not wanted?"

"Don't be insulting the man," Jess said. "From what Melody and Harmony say, he helped save both of them from that bastard Decker. Any man who will do that is all right in my book. We'll let him go his way in peace."

Fargo tried one last time. "I'm not going anywhere until I've seen the Britches. Or at least Maude. Go ask her if I can. I'll wait here."

Jess shook his head. "No, you're leaving, now." He nudged his horse to within an arm's length of where Fargo knelt. "Wes and me will escort you down the road a piece to be sure you don't get any ideas about sneaking on back."

Letting his shoulders slump as if resigned to obeying, Fargo put his hands on the ground to push to his feet. He scooped dirt into his left palm but left his right free. Then, as he straightened, he flung the dirt at Jess's horse while at the same time he seized the rope with his other hand and whipped it at Wesley's animal.

The two horses shied, Jess's bucking so high it threw him. Wesley's horse whinnied and whirled so swiftly he almost fell off.

Fargo took a bound and grabbed the back of Wesley's shirt. With a sharp heave he hurled the younger man to the earth with such force that Wesley lay stunned. Spinning, Fargo reached Jess before Jess could stand, and he punched him in the stomach. Jess sputtered and doubled over. Fargo gripped Jess's shirt, prepared to beat some sense into him if need be, when the air cracked to the retort of a rifle and a slug bit into the dirt inches from his right boot.

"That'll be enough, stranger, unless you're looking to die."

8

The speaker was a magnificent redhead dressed in men's clothing; a baggy flannel shirt, loose jeans, and brown boots. Despite her apparel, her stunning figure was a treasure to behold. She had piercing green eyes and a complexion bronzed to a golden tone by the sun. "I don't like to see anyone beat up on my boys. Ordinarily I'd have put a slug into you without thinking twice, but I saw how they treated you so for the moment I'll give you the benefit of the doubt." The woman got down off her horse. "I'm Primalia Harper, by the way. Folks generally call me Prima."

Fargo released Jess, who sank to a knee gasping for air. He told her his name, adding, "All I want to do is talk to the Britches. It's important. But your boys wouldn't see it that way."

"They can be a mite pigheaded at times," Prima said. "But they're men, so the condition is to be expected." She walked up to Wesley and poked him with her toe. "On your feet, you ornery whelp. Later we're having a long talk about the proper way to greet strangers."

"Ah, Ma," Wesley said, rising gingerly, a hand pressed to his lower back. "We just wanted to teach him a lesson. We wouldn't have hurt him none."

"How was Mr. Fargo to know that?" Prima retorted. "From the looks of him, he could bust both your thick heads without working up a sweat. You're lucky he was feeling charitable."

Fargo brushed dirt from his buckskins while ogling her figure on the sly. She was as fine-looking a female as he had ever come across, and it surprised him that she appeared to be in her early thirties. To his amazement, she caught his look and read his mind.

"I had these dunderheads when I was in my early teens," Prima said. "Figured I'd get the childbearing out of the way early so I could enjoy life with my husband. Then he had to go and get his fool head stove in by a horse. It's enough to make a body think there isn't any justice in this world."

"A woman like you should have no trouble marrying again," Fargo mentioned.

"Not likely. I've had my fill of men for a while. My husband, bless his soul, was a good provider but the dullest man in all of Oregon Territory and California besides."

"Ma!" Jess protested.

"Well, it's true, son," Prima said. "Your father hardly spoke two hundred words to me all the years we were married. I got so I'd talk to myself just to hold a conversation with someone."

Jess stood, flustered. "If Pa was that bad, why'd you marry him?"

Prima grinned. "He had other virtues that appealed to me when I was young. As I got older they didn't seem half so important as being able to do more than mumble a few syllables now and again."

Fargo received another surprise when she lowered her rifle and offered her hand. Her shake was as firm as any man's. "Thanks for not shooting me," he said.

"Thanks for not shooting them," Prima said. "I was too far off to stop them from making jackasses of themselves but I got here as quickly as I could."

Jess was rubbing his abdomen. "You were out riding?"

"No, I was out looking for the two of you. I told you to watch the road in case Decker's men showed, but when I looked through the spyglass I couldn't see you anywhere. So I came searching." Prima let down the hammer on her rifle. "Where did you two get to this time, as if I can't guess?"

"We just went up the road a ways," Wesley said, looking guiltily at his brother.

"That's all," Jess confirmed.

Prima turned to Fargo. "I wouldn't believe these two if they swore on the Good Book. Are they telling the truth or not?"

The Harper boys glanced at Fargo in alarm, their eyes begging him not to reveal the truth. He glanced at the rope, still lying on the ground, then ran a hand over his sore left elbow, and said, "If they are, then they have twins who were at Vereen's a short while ago."

"I knew it!" Prima declared, confronting her youngest. "What were you doing? Buying more sweets for Tune? How many times do I have to tell you that she's too young for you? At the rate you're going, all her teeth will rot out before she's marrying age."

"She's only three years younger than me," Jess objected. "Pa was seven years older than you so I don't see why you're so upset."

Prima gestured in exasperation. "Get to the house, both of you. I'll be along shortly."

Fargo walked toward the Ovaro and the redhead joined him, leading her mount. "It sounds to me like those boys are almost more than you can handle," he said.

"They're trying at times but I wouldn't trade being their mother for all the gold in Colorado," Prima said. "Jess reminds me a lot of me when I was his age, and Wesley is the spitting image of his father."

"I heard that you're from Arkansas," Fargo said to make small talk.

"My husband was. I'm from Kansas, myself. Met Ed in Kansas City and fell in love at first sight. My parents tried to talk me out of going off with him but of course I wouldn't listen." Prima chuckled, the sound like a deep, throaty purr. "Makes me wonder how any of us live past twenty."

Fargo took advantage of the opening. "If Abe Decker has his way, Tune Britches won't. And the rest of her family will be pushing up moss too."

Prima said nothing until they were at the stallion. "What's your interest in all of this? We were told that you saved two of the sisters from Decker's crowd, but the Britches hardly know you."

"Do you think I'd be smart to just ride off, like your sons want me to do?" Fargo asked.

"I didn't say that," Prima replied. "The Britches can use all the help they can get, whether they're too stubborn to admit it or not. Abe Decker isn't the type of man to forgive and forget. He won't stop until he's planted them."

"Why?" Fargo inquired, hoping at long last he would learn the real reason.

"I can't say. I gave my word I'd hold my tongue, and I pride myself on always keeping my word."

Fargo mounted. She did the same, her movements as lithe and graceful as a panther's. It didn't take a genius to see that Prima Harper was an exceptional woman who could hold her own anywhere, anytime. "The Britches are here, aren't they?" he said as they walked to the road and then brought their animals to a trot.

"They're supposed to be in hiding," Prima said. "My boys brought them over the other day. We mixed their horses with a string the boys were leading, thinking it might throw Decker off the scent."

"Decker isn't your main worry. He's hired a man named Vic Dunn who has spent the last ten to twelve years murdering people for a living. Dunn is the one you need to watch out for. He'll kill anyone who stands in his way."

"We've heard about him," Prima said. "Thought you were Dunn for a while."

The buildings and corral had been well maintained. Often when farmers and ranchers died, their wives were so heartbroken they let their homes go to ruin from neglect. Not so the Harper spread. Prima and her sons had a place anyone would be proud to own.

Fargo noted this as he dismounted next to a hitching post near the two-story log house. The brothers stood on the porch, glaring. He ignored them and scanned the buildings. "So where are you hiding your guests?" he asked.

Prima walked to a pair of red root cellar doors on the west side of the house. She knocked twice, then lifted the right-hand door. "Maude, Leland, come on out. You have company calling."

The mother poked her head out first. Maude showed no surprise on seeing Fargo, and even gave him a friendly smile. "Well, Mr. Fargo. You keep showing up where I least expect you to. Did you miss us so much you couldn't stay away?"

Fargo took her hand as she climbed the last step. "You're in trouble and I'd like to help. It's as simple as that."

The next moment Leland exploded from the cellar, his hand

on the revolver wedged under his belt. "You again!" he roared. "I don't know who you are and I don't give a damn! I want you to leave my family be or so help me, you're in for it!"

Maude wagged a finger at her husband. "Shush, Leland Britches. Can't you see Mr. Fargo is trembling in his boots, you have him so scared?"

Her sarcasm only made the man madder. Leland planted himself in front of Fargo and said, "Give me one good reason why I should let you within two feet of my brood?"

"Because you don't want any of them to die."

The others were piling out. First came Harmony, who turned her nose up in the air on seeing Fargo and walked off to avoid talking to him. Next came Melody, helped by Tune. Last to appear was Sym, who climbed the stairs slowly, her face giving no clue to her feelings.

Fargo had no warning of her intentions. Since she was behaving herself, he turned to say something to Prima, and it was then that Sym struck. She simply lowered her head and charged, catching Fargo in the hips with her broad shoulders. He landed on his back with her astraddle him and tried to grab her wrists to keep her from pounding him. Her right hand swung high, and in it was a dagger.

The barrel of a rifle suddenly blossomed in front of the big woman's face and Prima Harper said coolly, "That will be enough out of you, Sym. The man is my guest. Put that knife away and try to act like a lady for once."

Sym Britches had the look of a rabid dog. She froze, her fleshy features quivering with rage. "He hurt me, twice! No man does that to me and lives!"

"I won't tell you again," Prima said, cocking her weapon. "I'd hate to have to shoot you but I will if you leave me no choice."

For a second it seemed that Sym would try to stab Fargo anyway. Then, cursing under her breath, she slowly stood and moved to one side. "This isn't over between us, little man," she warned. "I'll see you in hell for what you did."

Fargo rose and picked up his hat. As if he did not have enough to deal with, now he needed to watch his back whenever Sym was around. "I'll get right to the point," he said, facing Maude and Leland. "Vic Dunn has arrived. It won't be long before he starts picking you off, one by one. I'll help you, if you'll let me."

"What can you do against a hardcase like him?" Leland asked. "They say he can pick off a man from a mile away." He anxiously glanced across the pasture. "For all we know he might be fixing a bead on one of us right this second."

"I doubt he knows where you are yet. In a day or so you can start to worry," Fargo said. "In the meantime you need a plan. And you need somewhere else to stay."

"What's wrong with right here?" Leland asked suspiciously. "Prima is our friend. She's trustworthy."

"She's also dead if Dunn learns she's sheltering you," Fargo said. "He's killed women before, even children. For Prima's sake, and the sake of her two boys, you should leave."

Maude had been hanging on every word. "But we have nowhere else to go, Mr. Fargo. We can't just camp out in the trees, not with Indians and wild beasts roaming the country-side."

"I agree," Prima interjected. "They can stay in the cellar for as long as they want. I'm willing to take the risk."

"Are you willing to risk Jess and Wesley?" Fargo challenged. "Because if Dunn thinks he can get at the Britches through them, he will. You could end up burying them beside your husband."

No one had a response to that. Fargo walked to a pump to give them time to talk it over. He worked the lever, then cupped his hand under the flow. The cold water was delicious.

"May I have some?"

Melody had followed him. She sipped a handful, then dabbed water on her neck and cheeks. "It gets awful stuffy down in that root cellar. Being cramped in there with my kin is enough to drive me loco." Her shoulder had been neatly bandaged and her left arm was in a sling.

"All the more reason to find somewhere else," Fargo said.

"I wish I knew where to go." Melody looked back to be sure no one else was close enough to overhear. Grinning impishly, she leaned close enough for Fargo to smell her hair. "Don't think I've forgotten about showing you how sorry I am for the terrible way I treated you before. As soon as I can, I aim to apologize properly."

"I can hardly wait," Fargo whispered. Over by the cellar Leland Britches was arguing with his wife and Prima. The color that flushed the redhead's cheeks when she was angry only added to her beauty.

"Fond of her, are you?" Melody asked, sounding a bit jealous.

"You can't fault a man for admiring a thoroughbred," Fargo said.

"Well, you can forget it," Melody said. "She hasn't shown any interest at all in men since her husband died. Lord knows, there have been enough gentlemen callers. She's the most eligible widow in these parts, having a grand ranch and all."

The argument had reached its climax. "Like hell I am!" Leland roared at the women. "It's my girls I'm thinking of." Hitching at his belt, he stomped off.

Maude shook her head, then glanced at Fargo. "It's the same old story. His brain works about as fast as a rock crawls uphill. Give him an hour to think and he'll see the light."

"Meanwhile, let's eat," Prima suggested. "I have a roast in the oven and I'd hate to see all that prime meat go to waste." She shocked the other women by taking Fargo's arm. "A man your size must have the appetite of a grizzly."

"In more ways than one," Fargo said.

The ranch house was as well kept inside as out. Spacious, comfortably furnished, it was so clean they could have eaten off the floor. Prima steered Fargo to one end of a long table and hung his hat on a rack. Both Harmony and Melody were agitated by the attention she bestowed on him but neither voiced an objection.

Fargo stretched out his legs and relaxed while the women prepared the meal. Since he had the time to spare, he asked Prima if she had a cleaning kit and spent the next half an hour cleaning his Colt. He was about done when Wesley Harper took a seat on his right.

"Mind if we talk, mister?"

"It's your house," Fargo reminded him.

"I hope there are no hard feelings about earlier. Jess and I thought you might mean to do the Britches harm."

"No hard feelings," Fargo said. A thought occurred to him and he leaned back in the chair. "Your family has lived here quite a while, haven't they?"

"Pretty near ten years now. Why?"

"I remember how I was at your age. Always on the go. You must have explored every square foot of your ranch and all the surrounding mountains besides."

"My brother and I have. Pa used to take us for long hikes all the time when we were small. He filled us with a love for the outdoors."

"Then maybe you know somewhere we can hide the Britches until this is over. A cave, an old cabin, somewhere they could be comfortable?" Fargo said.

Wesley scratched his chin. "Let me think. The closest thing to a cave in these parts is the grotto over in Grizzly Gulch." He paused. "There is a cabin up on Bald Mountain. It belonged to a prospector years ago. The roof is gone and one of the walls, so it wouldn't do to live in."

"Nothing else you know of?"

Jess Harper, who had been leaning against the stone fireplace and trying to admire Tune on the sly without being caught by her mother, chimed in, saying, "What about that old sawmill over by Darby Creek? It's still got a roof."

"Old mill?" Fargo said.

"A big old place," Wesley said. "My pa told us it was built by a rich Scotsman back in the fur days. The Scot was going to build his own fort and town and everything, and set himself up as the lord of the place, sort of like McLoughlin did up north. But the trade dried up and he ran out of money. All that's left is the sawmill."

"How far is it?"

"Oh, about ten miles, give or take."

Harmony came to the table. "I couldn't help hearing. And if you think I'm going to spend a night in that dreadful place, think again."

"Why not?" Fargo asked.

"It's dark and drafty, for one thing," Harmony said. "The floor is covered with dust inches thick and there are spiderwebs everywhere. It's probably crawling with black widows. I wouldn't be able to sleep a wink for fear one of them would crawl into my clothes."

Wesley's face lit up. "What I wouldn't give to be a black widow!"

Laughing, Harmony playfully squeezed his chin and pecked him on the tip of his nose. "When you can shave, come pay me a visit. If you're real lucky, and Pa doesn't carve you into bits, I might consent to going for a ride with you."

The reminder brought Fargo to his feet. He donned his hat and went to the door. "I'll check on Leland."

A breeze had sprung up, rustling the oak trees in the front yard. The afternoon sun was on its downward arc, casting long shadows, Out in the field cows lowed. By the stable chickens scratched in the dirt, clucking to themselves.

Fargo made a circuit of the house but did not see the father. A grove of apple trees had been planted fifty yards from the back door, and thinking that Britches had gone there to be by himself, Fargo went too. He wanted a chance to be alone with Leland, to attempt one more time to get the man to see reason. Leland's help would come in handy if he was going to tangle with Dunn and Decker's bunch, both.

The apple trees were spaced so closely that the grove was already shrouded in deep shadow. Fargo cupped his mouth to call out but thought better of the idea. He wasn't one of Leland's favorite people. The man might shoot rather than be persuaded to talk.

Strolling along a narrow path, Fargo was bothered by the silence around him. There should be birds frolicking among the trees, he mused, yet the grove was as lifeless as a graveyard. Out of habit he loosened the Colt in its holster. He didn't think Dunn had had enough time to meet with Decker, go to the Gulch, and follow the horse tracks to the Harper spread, but he wasn't about to underestimate the man. Vic Dunn's reputation was well deserved.

Fargo went the length of the grove and saw no one. He was about to turn and go back when he spied clods of earth at the northwest corner. They turned out to be fresh tracks, four horses that had ridden off to the west within the hour.

There were a few footprints. One set had been made by a rider who had briefly dismounted. Another had been made by

92

someone who stepped from the grove. The second man, who had to have been Leland Britches, had not gone back, which told Fargo that Leland had either been forced onto one of the horses at gunpoint or had gone with the riders of his own free will. Whichever, it deserved investigation.

Fargo jogged to the Ovaro. As he turned the stallion, the front door swung wide and out stepped Prima.

"You're leaving?" She sounded greatly disappointed.

"Leland might be in trouble. Keep everyone here." Fargo spurred the pinto to a lope. He knew the fresh tracks would join the road at some point and they did, less than a hundred yards from the woodland. The four men had been riding hard. One of the horses dug its hooves in deeper than the rest, showing that it carried two men.

Fargo was halfway to the trading post before the quartet came into sight on a flat stretch below the hill he was descending. He angled closer to the pines so they wouldn't catch a glimpse of him. They had slowed to a walk, confident they had gotten safely away.

Plunging into the brush, Fargo swung in a wide loop to the south, then west. If he could get in front of them, he'd have the element of surprise and might be able to take Leland without a fight. Provided the crusty old man wanted to go.

It was a brutal ride. The slopes of the hills were steep, the undergrowth thick. Frequently he had to make detours. He'd been cut, torn, and nicked by the time he turned back to the road and halted behind a row of pines. Vaulting down, he grounded the reins, drew his Colt, and crept close to the edge of the forest. He had done it. Several hundred yards to the east were the riders.

Cocking the Colt, Fargo flattened. He pulled grass and weeds loose and tossed them onto his back and the backs of his legs. By then the group was close enough for him to recognize Brickman and Rand. Touching his chin to the grass, he held himself still. But only for a few seconds. Hooves pounded to the west as someone approached from the post.

Fargo looked, and cursed his luck.

It was Abe Decker and Vic Dunn.

9

Skye Fargo had to lie completely still. The lumberjacks were unlikely to notice him, but Dunn had the instincts of a wild beast and was bound to notice anything out of the ordinary. The slightest movement would merit his attention.

As fate would have it, the two parties met almost directly in front of where Fargo lay concealed. Abe Decker dismounted. Leland Britches, after hesitating a few moments, slid off the back of Rand's horse.

"All right, Decker, I'm here. Your men told me that you wanted to talk, just the two of us." Leland acted nervous and kept shifting his weight from one foot to the other. "They also gave me your word that I wouldn't be harmed."

"I won't lift a finger against you," Decker said, smiling smugly. "You have my solemn promise on that."

"Then let's get to the meat of the matter," Leland said. "Why'd you send them to fetch me on the sly?"

Fargo saw Dunn scanning both sides of the road and wondered if the man was simply being cautious or whether Dunn sensed that something was wrong, that someone else was nearby.

Decker folded his arms and moved a few feet to the side of the road nearest Fargo. He turned, his back to the trees. "I sent them so I could offer you this one last chance to see things my way. Come to your senses, old man, before it's too late."

The crusty miner laughed. "Who are you trying to kid, mister? I know the real reason. You're worried because of what happened at your place. Those men building your fancy mansion saw Harmony get shot. I know. She told me." Leland chuckled. "Word will spread now, Decker. You can't keep it secret any longer." He made a gesture of contempt at Dunn.

94

"You'll have to send your hired vermin home. He can't very well kill us now, can he?"

"You think you know it all, don't you?" Decker said, an edge to his tone. "Well, you're not as smart as you think, Leland. I told the men who saw the shooting that I never wanted your daughter harmed. That it was all a misunderstanding." He paused. "Then I fired the idiot who pulled the trigger. And guess what? On his way out of the valley, he was killed by the man who pretended to be Dunn—"

"Fargo, you mean," Leland said.

Fargo had half a mind to shoot the miner himself. He'd hoped Dunn wouldn't learn his identity until it was too late. Now the man would be doubly cautious and twice as deadly. As if to accent the thought, the killer stiffened.

"What name did you say?"

"Fargo, he called himself," Leland clarified. "Skye Fargo. Why?"

Vic Dunn had the look of a coiled rattler about to strike. "Skye Fargo," he repeated roughly. "That explains a lot. What the hell is he doing in this territory?"

"Do you know him?" Decker asked.

"I know *of* him," Dunn said, "and he's not a man to take lightly. He's almost as good as I am. He could give us trouble."

Leland glanced sharply at Decker. "What's he mean by that? Didn't you hear me? You can't lay a finger on my family now or you'll wind up hung."

"You think so?" Decker shook his head. "Before the law hangs someone, they need proof a crime was done. And I'm not about to give them that proof." He lowered his arms. "The only ones who knows what I'm up to are the men here and one other. Vereen knows I sent for Dunn, but I paid him well to keep his mouth shut and he knows better than to cross me."

"The workers at your place—?" Leland said.

"They saw how upset I was when Harmony was wounded. They saw me kick Terrell off my land."

Leland lost some of his bluster. He jabbed a finger at Dunn, saying, "And what about him? How will you explain this bastard off?"

"I don't need to. A man your age should know how the law

95

works. They'd need to prove I hired him before I could be charged," Decker said.

"That's right," Dunn chipped in. "They'd have to catch me first and that will never happen."

Worry made Leland swallow hard, his Adam's apple bobbing. "Hold on here. I came because you gave your word I wouldn't come to any harm."

Fargo placed his thumb on the hammer of his Colt. He would try to help Britches if Decker attempted to kill him.

"I'm making you this final offer," the timber king was saying. "I'm willing to overlook the insult. I'm willing to overlook the rest of it. All you have to do is persuade her to become my wife."

"I can't do that," Leland said. "My girls all have minds of their own. She'd never listen."

"You're her father. Convince her it's in her own best interest, in the interests of your whole family." Decker's next words were snapped out in bitter resentment. "After all, you take pride in sticking together, don't you? In helping one another out?"

Leland rubbed his palms on his dirty pants. He licked his lips, then braced his shoulders. "No deal, Decker. Marrying you is about the worst thing that could happen to one of my girls. You're mean as a snake, mister, and no-account to boot. You'd make a terrible husband."

"And you're perfect, I suppose?" Decker taunted, moving to his horse. "Fair enough, you old bastard. I've tried for the last time. And the only reason I did is because I still feel for her, believe it or not. I'm not the heartless son of a bitch you think I am." Decker jabbed a finger at the miner. "But I won't be made a fool of, not by any man, certainly not by a bunch of women. I'll see—"

A shot rang out and the back of Leland's head exploded in a spray of gore. The impact of the slug flung him onto his back, his arms outflung, his eyes gaping wide.

Fargo had been watching Decker, waiting for him to go for his gun or to signal Vic Dunn. He was as taken aback by the gunshot as the rest appeared to be.

"What the hell!" Decker roared at the killer. "I wasn't done talking!"

Dunn lifted his smoking Colt and blew on the end of the barrel. "Relax, Abe," he said, as a man might address a contrary child. "You told me to kill him if he refused, and he refused, didn't he? I just got tired of hearing the two of you flap your gums."

Fargo decided to avenge the old miner and put a stop to the bloodshed before any of the women became victims. He slowly pulled his knees toward his chest so he could jump to his feet and cut loose, but he had no more than moved his legs a foot when Vic Dunn whirled in his direction.

"There! Skye Fargo! Kill him!"

Fargo rolled to the left in the nick of time. Dunn fanned his pistol twice so swiftly the two shots were as one, the slugs smacking into the earth at the very spot Fargo had vacated. He surged to his knees to blast at Dunn but the wily killer slipped onto the far side of the calico, hanging Indian fashion, and squeezed off another shot from under the animal's neck. The bullet clipped Fargo's shirt but didn't draw any blood. Meanwhile, Decker's men finally overcame their surprise and added their guns to the din.

Faro had no choice but to hurl himself into the brush and run. Slugs ripped into the vegetation on either side and drilled into the dirt at his feet. He saw the four lumberjacks wheel their horses into the woods after him and snapped off a shot to deter them. One ducked low and tried to swing onto the off side of his mount as Dunn had done but lost his grip and dangled from the stirrup.

Dunn's Sharps boomed just as Fargo reached the pines. He had darted to the left to cut between two of them and the slug missed him by a whisker and tore a chunk out of one of the trunks. In two more long strides Fargo reached the Ovaro and vaulted into the saddle.

The lumberjacks were closing in from the right, Dunn from the left. Their shots peppered the landscape, some much too close for comfort.

Fargo applied his reins and spurs and galloped due south. He hunched low over the stallion's neck, concerned the poor aim of the timbermen would result in the pinto being hit. Weaving furiously among the trees, he made it as hard for his pursuers as he could. A clear shot at one of them presented itself but he had to hold his fire as the very next instant the man was hidden by trees.

Coming to a bluff, Fargo reined up to check the slope below. There were too many ruts for him to risk taking it at top speed. Veering to the right, he rode along the crest until he came to a spine that angled down into a meadow. Fargo raced to the bottom, then skirted the open space, preferring to ride along the edge of the forest.

Seconds later Dunn and the other four arrived in a flurry of hoofbeats. Dunn spotted him immediately and led the others on.

Fargo knew he wouldn't shake a man like Dunn easily. Besides being an expert tracker, Dunn had a fine horse, a worthy equal of the Ovaro. Both could gallop for miles on end and not tire out. And both could go without water for three times as long as the average mount.

One of Decker's men stupidly banged off several pistol shots although the range was far too great. Fargo kept one eye on Dunn, who held the Sharps. It was well he did, for as he came to the end of the meadow and sped in among a stand of madrones, Dunn fired. Again the killer missed, but only by a paper's width. It was an excellent shot, given that Dunn was speeding along at a full gallop.

Fargo knuckled down to serious riding. He shoved the Colt in his holster, gripped the reins in both hands, and concentrated on avoiding deadfalls and solitary logs. A rolling series of steep mountains brought him to a wide plain dominated by a butte. When he looked back he saw Dunn and two others on the crest of the last mountain. The other pair had already given up.

The butte became Fargo's goal. From there he would have a clear shot and be able to pick off the scourge of the Northwest and Decker's boys as they crossed the plain. He relaxed a little, thinking things had finally gone his way. With Dunn taken care of, Decker would soon follow. The Britches would be safe and he could go on to California. Or maybe he'd spend some time at the Harper ranch. Prima was worth a delay.

Bordering the butte were jagged gullies, many lined with brush. They slowed Fargo, forcing him to pick his way carefully in order to avoid a misstep that could prove fatal to the pinto and put him at Dunn's mercy. Down one slope and up another he went, loose gravel and stones sliding out from under the stallion, thorny limbs tearing at both of them.

At the last gully before the butte, Fargo drew rein and turned in the saddle. He expected to see the three men a third of the way onto the plain, at least, yet there was no sign of them. Nor were they visible on the mountain.

Fargo rode to the bottom of the gully and swung down. Yanking the Sharps out, he hurried to the rim where he knelt and fed a round into the rifle. He quickly adjusted the rear sight for a distance of five hundred yards and hunkered down to await his enemies.

But something was wrong. Neither Dunn nor the timbermen appeared. Fargo wondered if they had also given up and gone on back to Decker. Moments later he spotted the two lumberjacks climbing the mountain. Vic Dunn wasn't with them.

The explanation was obvious. Fargo realized the killer was stalking him. He didn't see how Dunn could get close enough to shoot, not across that flat, barren plain, but he was taking no chance. Descending, he led the pinto by the reins to a different spot a hundred yards up the gully.

From his new vantage point, Fargo could see for miles in all directions except due south, where the rugged butte towered hundreds of feet skyward. It was too sheer to climb so he wasn't worried about Dunn circling around and firing down on him from its lofty heights.

Another factor worked in Fargo's favor. The sun was half gone. Once it was dark he could forget about Dunn and head for the ranch. By morning he would have the Britches safely tucked away at the old sawmill.

The breeze grew stronger, fanning the dust. Fargo pushed his hat back and knelt on one knee to relieve a cramp in his other leg. He glanced at the sun, wishing it would sink all the way, and the next thing he knew, he was lying on his back on the gully slope listening to the faint retort of a heavy-caliber rifle.

For a few seconds Fargo lay stunned, hardly able to accept the fact that he had just been shot. An explosion of pain confirmed it, agony racking him from ear to ear. He reached up, touched his left temple, and felt his finger grow slick with warm blood.

Then the reaction hit him. A churning in Fargo's gut made him feel as if he would retch. Gritting his teeth, he held the contents of his stomach down and slowly rose to his hands and knees. The world swam and blurred. A bush right in front of him seemed to be under six feet of water.

Fargo fought the vertigo and stood. His legs threatened to buckle as a cloud passed before his eyes. Shaking his head, he dug in his boots and stood firm. He had to get out of there. Dunn would be coming for him, and in his weakened state he'd be no match for the killer.

Through a milky fog Fargo saw his Sharps lying a few feet away. He took a halting step and bent to pick it up. Suddenly the ground rushed up to meet his face and the pain flooded through him from head to toe.

For over a minute Fargo made no attempt to rise. He waged an internal war, fighting a tide of darkness that tried to strip him of his consciousness. He knew if he went under he would never wake up. Dunn wound find him and kill him.

The Ovaro nickered, as if in warning. Fargo struggled to sit up, grasped the Sharps in both hands, and, using it as a crutch, shoved to his feet. He saw the stallion with head high, staring out over the plain. With an effort he turned his head and spied his hat lying below the rim.

Fargo climbed, each step a labor of sheer will. He had to squat to grip the hat. If he bent over, he felt he might not rise again. Once he had it on, he peeked above the rim. Four hundred yards out was Vic Dunn, rushing toward the gully.

Fargo knew that he couldn't hit the broad side of a barn if it was right in front of him, but he had to discourage Dunn long enough for him to take flight. It took all his strength to lift the Sharps. When he took a bead, he realized there were two Dunns, not one. Try as he might, he couldn't make up his mind which was the killer and which wasn't. So he aimed between the two, then fired.

Something happened that had never happened before. The recoil of the big .52 lifted Fargo clear off his feet and sent him tumbling down into the gully. He stopped rolling only when his shoulder hit a small tree. Or he assumed it was a tree until the Ovaro's face dipped toward his head and he felt its moist muzzle touch his lips.

Fargo weakly pushed the pinto's head aside, hooked an arm around its front leg, and rose. The Sharps was right beside him. Holding on to the stallion to keep from pitching over, he retrieved the rifle and shoved it into the scabbard. The effort exhausted him. He listened but didn't hear the calico. That would soon change. Dunn wasn't the type to lay low for long.

The saddle horn seemed much higher than it ever had before. Fargo gripped it as firmly as his weakened limbs allowed, then pulled. To his dismay he barely lifted himself an inch. Girding his shoulders, he tried again with little better success.

The Ovaro gave a low whinny.

Fargo didn't need to look to know that Dunn was on his way. The thought that he would be dead in a few minutes unless he forced his body to obey his will lent him the strength he needed to awkwardly climb into the saddle. Once on, he nearly collapsed and had to clutch the horn like a rank greenhorn to keep from slipping off.

A tap of the heels was all it took to goad the dependable stallion into motion. Fargo stayed in the gully. Bent low, his legs clamped tight, he brought the pinto to a trot. Ordinarily the rocking motion had no more effect on him than would the motion of a rocking chair. This time it caused his surroundings to spin and dance and his stomach to flip-flop.

In the distance, hoofs hammered.

Fargo figured Dunn was still two hundred yards out. He rode faster, his insides churning worse, his palms growing slick with sweat. He could barely hold on. When the Ovaro went around a turn, he was swung to the right so violently that one hand slipped loose. He had to press hard against the stirrups or he would have landed on his face.

A straight stretch appeared. Fargo kept one hand on the saddle horn, another entwined in the pinto's mane, and increased his speed to a gallop. Bile rose in his mouth and he spat it out. The wind on his face helped some but not enough to fully restore him.

When he was almost to the next bend, Fargo risked a look

back. Dunn wasn't in sight yet. More encouraging was the fact that the sun had nearly set. Twilight had descended, and before long it would be too dark for Dunn to track him. All he had to do was stay alive until then and he would be safe.

Abruptly, the gully ended in a short slope. Fargo drew rein and promptly regretted it. For some reason he felt sicker than ever simply sitting still. Flicking the reins, he went up the slope at a walk, his head pounding so loudly he could barely hear himself think. Once at the top he gave the Ovaro its head.

Fargo had to hug the saddle with all his might to stay on the pinto. He felt something on his cheek and realized with a start that blood covered half of his face, his jaw, and his neck. Since he dared not stop to examine the wound, he could only hope he wasn't slowly bleeding to death.

Fargo had no idea how far he had gone when he heard a bellow of frustration. Vic Dunn had just ridden out of the gully and spotted him. The killer's Sharps belched lead and smoke but Dunn rushed his shot and missed. Fargo felt too feeble to return fire. He was content to race on into the gathering darkness, his goal the haven offered by the forest at the end of the plain.

Dunn raked his calico with his spurs, giving chase.

Whether Fargo lived or died now depended on the Ovaro. The sturdy stallion had to outrace the superb mare, and even though the Ovaro had a large lead, Fargo knew it would be no easy task. He was proven right before the first minute had gone by. The mare put on a spurt of speed the likes of which he had seldom witnessed, cutting his lead by a third. He could see dust flying out from under her lightning hooves, and the confident smirk Dunn wore.

Fargo concentrated on riding and forgot about them for a while. Slowly he regained some of his strength, enough for him not to worry about falling. His main worry was his head, the torment being so severe he bit his lower lip to keep from crying out.

Across the barren plain the two horses sped, the smaller mare gaining bit by bit. Vic Dunn reloaded but held his fire, waiting until he was close enough to be sure. Fargo tried once to pull his rifle free but couldn't quite get it all the way out. He regretted having stuck it in the scabbard but knew he would have long since tumbled from the saddle had he burdened himself with the Sharps.

Second by second the sky darkened. The rosy belt rimming the western horizon faded to a dull pink, then to blue, and finally to black. A few stars sparkled in the heavens, their number growing as time went by.

After half a mile the mare was only three hundred yards behind the stallion. Over the next quarter mile she gained a piddling few yards. Thereafter, she lost ground, and by the time the inky wall of forest loomed ahead of Fargo, the mare was more than four hundred yards away.

It was Fargo's turn to smirk. The Ovaro had served him in good stead once again. He was within a stone's throw of the tree when Dunn fired out of desperation. The leaden hornet buzzed harmlessly past, and the following instant Fargo galloped into the woods. As the vegetation closed around him he cut to the right, went fifty yards, then cut to the left.

To Fargo's rear, limbs cracked and brush crackled. Vic Dunn was not even trying to exercise stealth. The killer wanted Fargo in the worst way and had thrown caution to the wind.

Suddenly a large log barred the Ovaro's path and without being prodded the stallion vaulted it in a smooth leap. Fargo thought he was braced for the landing but the jolt nearly threw him. He clutched the fork with one hand and the cantle with the other to stop himself from losing his seat.

It sounded as if Dunn were gaining again. In the forest the small mare had a big advantage in being able to weave faster and to go through narrow gaps the Ovaro instinctively avoided.

Fargo still had high hopes he would escape. He had to get to the Harper spread and warn Prima. Decker knew the Britches were at her place and would lose no time in closing in. Fargo made himself a promise that if Decker harmed one red hair on Prima's pretty head, he was going to shoot Decker to pieces.

Deep in thought when he shouldn't be, Fargo paid hardly any attention to the trees streaking past. He was counting on the Ovaro to avoid all obstacles. So he didn't see the low hanging limb until it was too late. He felt the impact, though, felt it for a fleeting second of extreme agony, just before the stars blinked out, the trees vanished, and he was swept into a great black emptiness.

10

The chattering of an agitated squirrel brought Skye Fargo back to the world of the living. He was on his back, staring up at a pine tree. High overhead sat the gray squirrel, tail twitching without letup as it chided Fargo for having the audacity to invade its domain.

"Shut up," Fargo growled, thinking the noise would lead Dunn to him. Then he saw that it was daylight and realized he had been out all night long.

Rolling on his side, Fargo paused. The simple movement had aggravated his head wound. It felt as if someone were beating on his skull with an iron mallet. He waited for the pain to taper off before sitting up.

The sun hung an hour high in the sky. Fargo glanced around, seeking Dunn, and instead found the Ovaro grazing a short distance off. Puzzled by the killer's absence, even more puzzled at being alive, Fargo carefully stood and took stock.

The limb had hit him flush across the brow. There was no blood and no gash marks. He was glad his hard head had survived intact but wouldn't care to go through the experience ever again. Coming on top of the gunshot, it was a miracle he could still think straight.

Fargo ran his fingers over the wound and discovered it had long since stopped bleeding. The furrow wasn't as deep as he had imagined it would be, and he doubted there would be a scar. He picked up his hat, then stood slowly so as not to bring on another attack of dizziness.

The Ovaro walked toward him, the reins dragging. Fargo took them in hand and mounted, again taking care not to move too rapidly. A persistent, gnawing headache bothered him, and his mouth felt as if he had licked a polecat clean with his tongue, but otherwise he was all right.

Fargo rode in a small circle, reading the sign. He located the tree limb that had laid him low and noticed how the Ovaro's tracks kept on bearing to the northeast. Paralleling them a few yards to the left were the mare's smaller hoofprints. Apparently Vic Dunn had ridden right on by after he had been knocked out, and not seen him in the dark. Dunn had chased the Ovaro and had either given up when he realized that the stallion was riderless or because the Ovaro had gotten clean away.

"I owe you, big fella," Fargo said, giving the pinto an affectionate pat. "You pulled my bacon out of the fire again."

Fargo made for the Harper ranch without delay. He didn't like to think of all that could have happened while he was unconscious. Dunn might have gone there directly, and by now all the Britches and Harpers were buzzard bait. He pushed the stallion in order to reach the small valley by noon.

When still two miles from the ranch, Fargo spotted a thick column of smoke that added to his worry. He came to the road and took it the rest of the way. Once he galloped into the open he could see the charred ruins of the ranch house and the stable. Acting on the off chance Decker and company were still there, he drew his Colt and went down the road at a brisk walk.

The panicked cattle had all run off and were huddled in bunches near the hills. A few horses grazed to the north. Nothing else moved.

Fargo saw a body lying near the remains of the corral. He reined up, lowered himself, and stepped warily toward the victim, who lay facedown. It was a man, Fargo noted, and he hoped it was one of Decker's men. Using a boot, he flipped the body over.

Wesley Harper had taken three shots, once in the chest, once in the stomach, the third time above the left eye. Any one of them would have proven fatal. He must have died swiftly while on his way from the house to the stable, Fargo deduced, never knowing what had hit him.

Fargo went to the house, fearing he would find burnt corpses among the smoking timbers and beams. Fingers of flame still licked hungrily at piles of shattered, blistered wood. It was too hot for him to get very close, and he had to content himself with making a circuit around the perimeter. There were no other bodies that he could see, not so much as a single blackened skeleton.

The stable seemed his best bet. Fargo hurried over and scoured the burning debris. Several horses had perished in the flames and all that was left of them were mounds of putrid black flesh that resembled piles of melted wax. Near a rear corner lay a mass of bubbling hide and horns that had once been a prized bull. Scattered throughout the yard were the bodies of the chickens, their heads shot off.

Fargo was encouraged by the lack of human remains, but it left him wondering whether the rest had escaped or been taken alive by Decker. He tried to make sense of the jumbled overlapping tracks but there were too many, all going every which way.

Figuring he'd do better from horseback, Fargo hastened to the Ovaro. He started to replace his Colt but changed his mind on hearing an odd thump coming from the vicinity of the house. Moving around the stallion, he heard the thump repeated. He cocked the pistol and scoured the rubble, unable to pinpoint exactly where the sound came from.

Then it was repeated again. Fargo moved to the side of the house and saw the root cellar doors still intact, but the outer surfaces were the color of charcoal and a large beam had fallen across them. As he looked, someone pounded on the doors from below.

Fargo dashed over, shoved the Colt in his holster, and stooped to push. In his excitement he failed to take his condition into account. His head swam, his ears rung. He buckled down and pushed anyway, moving the heavy timber a few feet but not yet enough to open the doors.

From within came a terrified squeal, then rustling.

Going to his knees, Fargo shoved a third time. It was the charm. The beam slid off and he grabbed the metal handle. Instantly pain seared his palm. The metal was scalding hot. He removed his bandanna, wrapped it around his right hand, and tried once more. The heat was bearable. He threw the door wide and crouched. "Who's down here?"

No one answered.

Fargo leaned forward. The steps hadn't been so much as singed. The hole was hot, though, so hot it brought beads of sweat to his skin. He didn't see how anyone could have survived the inferno by taking shelter down there. "It's Fargo," he called out. "You have nothing to be afraid of."

Silence mocked him.

Fargo went down the stairs slowly, adjusting his eyes to the gloom. Two of the walls were lined with shelves containing preserves, and many of the jars had burst. A few tools hung from pegs on the third. To the right of the steps, in the corner farthest from the house, lay a pile of burlap bags. As Fargo turned toward them, they moved, quivering as if alive.

Fargo saw a gap in the layers. He hooked a hand under and heaved, tossing a dozen bags aside and exposing the frightened girl curled into a knot underneath. "Tune," he said softly.

Tuney Britches blinked at him, tears streaking her sooty face. "It's really you!" she blurted. "I thought it was Decker playing a trick!"

Fargo had barely straightened when she threw herself into his arms, sobbing hysterically. He stroked her long hair, saying, "It's all right. You're safe now." She cried harder, her whole body shaking, and continued to cry for the better part of five minutes.

To Fargo's surprise, he was oddly uncomfortable. It came from spending all his spare time in the company of grown women, he supposed. He couldn't remember the last time he'd been around a girl of Tune's tender years.

Sniffling, Tune drew back and wiped her nose with the back of her sleeve. "I'm sorry, Mr. Fargo. I've just been so scared. It's been awful. I thought I was going to die when they set the house on fire."

"Tell me about it outside," Fargo said, taking her hand. She stumbled going up the steps and he caught her before she fell. Once in the bright sunlight she blinked and glanced nervously toward the apple grove.

"That's where they came from, Decker and his men. They hit us after dark, when most of us were out on the porch getting the breeze and waiting for Pa and you to come back."

Tune gave a tiny gasp and clutched his arm. "Pa! Where is he? Why didn't you bring him?"

The budding fear in her eyes made Fargo hesitate. The last thing he wanted to do was break such terrible news to her, but he couldn't put it off. He placed a hand on her shoulder and said as tenderly as he knew how, "Vic Dunn killed him. I'm sorry. It happened so fast there was nothing I could do."

Tears poured from Tune's bloodshot eyes, but she didn't go into hysterics. Lips quivering, she clenched her small fists and bowed her pointed chin. "Oh, Lord," she breathed sadly. "I loved Pa so much."

Fargo turned away to give her time to be alone with her thoughts. At his first step, she gripped his elbow, her nails digging deep.

"Where are you going? Don't leave me alone, mister. Decker and that monster Dunn might come back. They'll be looking for those of us who got away."

Fargo would have liked to question her but held off in order not to upset her more than she already was. But one fact he had to learn. "Do you know where the others went?"

"No, sir," Tune said. "When the shooting started, I got so scared I couldn't think straight. Instead of going back into the house like the others, I ran around the side. The cellar doors were still open so I scooted down in and closed them. I reckon Decker's bunch never saw me or they would have drug me out and filled me full of lead."

"You couldn't have seen much from down there," Fargo remarked.

"No, I didn't. But I heard everything. I heard the screaming and shouting and all the guns going off. And I could hear my family and the Harpers talking up in the living room. I heard them say Jess and Harmony were hurt, and they were going to make a run for it. Wesley went out the door first to cover them. And then there was so much shooting—" Tune broke off, unable to finish.

Fargo needed to have some idea of how much time had gone by since the defenders had taken to the woods. "Were they trapped in the house very long?"

"Hours. Mostly it was quiet, except for the shooting. But later that man Dunn showed up, and he kept shouting, poking fun at Ma and Prima, calling the boys names and daring them to come out. He was enjoying himself, that man. He acted like it was a game." Tune sniffed. "I bet it was his notion to set the house on fire. He'd do something like that."

Fargo watched a finger of flame lick at a splintered pile of black wood that had once been the big table. "They can't have been gone very long," he said, half to himself.

"A little before dawn would be my guess," Tune said. "It wasn't long after they lit it out that I saw daylight through cracks in the door." She looked longingly into the distance. "I wish I'd gone with them."

A comment the girl had made stuck in Fargo's mind. "You said you were able to hear your family up in the house. If that's the case, they could have heard you. Why didn't you call out, let them know where you were?"

"I was afraid Decker would hear me." Tune began crying again. "I'm yellow, mister. A regular coward."

Fargo shook his head. "What else could you have done? Have you ever shot anyone?"

"No," Tune said meekly.

"Dunn has killed women and children before. He'd shoot you without a second thought." Patting her back, he added, "You did the smart thing. You survived." He walked toward the Ovaro and she tagged along, weeping softly. Suddenly she stopped, a hand over her mouth, gaping at Wesley's body.

"Oh, no! They killed poor Wes."

"Afraid so," Fargo said, reaching for the reins.

"Ain't you going to bury him, mister?"

"I hadn't planned on it." Fargo wanted to find the others and told her as much.

"But it ain't right, us going off and leaving Wes for the buzzards and varmints and such."

"He'll keep until we get back. It's not like he's going to go anywhere," Fargo said, and promptly regretted it when the girl commenced bawling in earnest.

"Please, Mr. Fargo?" she blubbered. "Wes was a powerful good friend of mine. He wasn't sweet on me like Jess, but he treated me real decent. I can't just go off and leave him to rot or be ate."

Hiding a scowl, Fargo let the reins drop and walked to the

dead man. The body had stiffened quite a bit and he had to dig in his boot heels to drag it over to a bare spot between the corral and the house. He remembered seeing tools down in the root cellar and went to see if a shovel was included. Secretly he hoped there wouldn't be so he'd have a good excuse to put the burying off. But there a long-handled shovel stood, propped in a dark corner.

Tune wore a grateful smile when Fargo emerged. He dug swiftly, scooping a shallow grave, and bent to flip Wesley into the hole.

"That's not big enough yet, is it?" Tune asked. "I mean, we wouldn't want the coyotes to come along and dig him up, would we? I think you should dig a couple of feet deeper."

Fargo looked at her. "One day you're going to make a perfect wife."

"Really?" Tune brightened even more. "Why, that's sweet of you to say. How can you be so sure, though?"

"Call it a hunch," Fargo said dryly as he returned to his digging. Fifteen minutes later he had the grave dug to the girl's satisfaction. Throwing down the shovel, he put his boot on Harper to roll the dead man in but stopped when Tune clucked like a riled hen and wagged a finger at him.

"Mr. Fargo! Is that any way to treat the departed? My ma says we ought to treat the deceased with respect. I think you should lift him down in."

"Care to help?" Fargo asked sourly.

"Me? I couldn't touch a dead person! It scares the daylights out of me just thinking about it."

Sighing, Fargo hopped into the grave, hooked his hands around Wesley's legs, and eased the young man into his final resting place. He scrambled back out and grabbed the shovel to fill in the hole, then heard Tune cluck again.

"Ain't we going to say a few words? That's the proper thing to do."

"You say them," Fargo said.

"But you're the grown-up. You should know all about the Good Book. Pick pretty words so Wes will be pleased."

"Wes is dead."

"That don't hardly matter. He can hear us up in heaven."

Fargo wondered how parents stayed sane. He disliked being

111

put on the spot but tried his best to think of something appropriate so the girl wouldn't set to blubbering again. The only phrase he could think of was, "Ashes to ashes, dust to dust." He saw her look of disapproval and went on, "He was a good boy, Lord. See he gets his due. And spare him from the worms."

"That's it?" Tune said when he stopped. "Goodness gracious. My ma could have done a lot better."

"We'll bring her back and have her say some words over him," Fargo said, bending. In short order he had the body covered and the dirt tamped down. Tossing the shovel aside, he climbed onto the Ovaro and held his hand out. "Let's go. There are only five hours of daylight left."

Tune swung lithely up and put her arms around his waist. "Your six-shooter is poking me in the arm," she complained.

"Then move your arm," Fargo said. Riding northward until he was past the smoldering house, he made a circuit of the burned-out structures and found where two riders had gone eastward with Decker's men in pursuit. To the south was another trail made by a single horse. That left three people unaccounted for. He made a sweep of the adjacent fields to be certain none had been gunned down while fleeing.

"Why are we taking so long?" Tune demanded. "If you know which way my ma went, let's go find her before it gets dark.

Fargo picked the likeliest trail. Since Decker wanted the Britches wiped out, he figured the timber king had gone after Maude and whoever rode with her. He traveled at a lope so as not to wear the Ovaro out after the long night of hard travel they had both been through.

The tracks crossed the small valley to thick woodland. Decker had been led on a merry chase deep into the mountains. One horse, smaller than the rest judging by the size of its hooves, had been in the lead the whole time. Dunn, Fargo figured, hankering for a chance to pay the killer back. Miles from the ranch Fargo topped a ridge and saw tendrils of smoke from a campfire far below.

"My ma, you think?" Tune asked hopefully.

"Could be," Fargo said, although he suspected it was really Decker's camp. Abe and his boys had been up all night and well into the new day. He feared they had caught Maude, finished her off, and were now resting.

"What are you waiting for?" Tune urged, slapping her legs against the stallion. "Get us down there!"

"Hold your britches on," Fargo commented, guiding the Ovaro into a line of oak trees. He descended until he was several hundred yards short of the camp, and downwind. After lowering Tune, he tugged on the Sharps and alighted. His head still bothered him but not nearly as severely as it had earlier.

"Let's go!" Tune said, stamping a foot. "Land sakes, you are the slowest thing on two legs! I had a turtle once that could outrun you and it spent most of its time hiding in its shell."

"You're staying with my horse," Fargo informed her. He raised a hand when she opened her mouth to protest. "We don't know if it is your mother. I'll go make sure it's safe."

"I don't want to be left alone," Tune said, eying the forest fearfully.

"A big girl like you can take care of herself," Fargo said.

"I thought I could too, until last night."

Fargo left, working his way through the undergrowth with the utmost care until he heard low voices and the rattle of tin cups. Parting a bush, he saw Abe Decker seated on a stump. Nearby squatted Vic Dunn. Rand and Brickman and two other lumberjacks were also present. So was a captive.

Jess Harper had been bound hand and feet and was on his knees near the fire. His hat was gone, his hair disheveled. He had been beaten black and blue, and dried blood rimmed his mouth and chin. His head hung low, his eyes were closed.

Lowering onto his elbows, Fargo flattened and crawled forward. He watched Dunn. Whenever the killer shifted or looked up, he froze. He was thirty feet away when Dunn stood and stretched, turning toward him in the process. Fargo curled his thumb around the hammer of the Sharps and coiled to leap up but Dunn merely yawned and sank back down.

Abe Decker was talking. ". . . need to use your head more and your guns less. The boy is bait, Dunn. So long as we have him, she won't try anything. We can use him, make her come to us. You'll see."

"I see a lot of things," Dunn said harshly. "I see that you let

113

yourself be outsmarted by a bunch of women and kids. I see that maybe hooking up with you was the wrong thing to do."

Decker gestured angrily with his coffee cup. "Hell, where were you when they were slipping away?"

"I shot that one, didn't I?" Dunn said. "I couldn't be everywhere at once."

"You let Fargo get away too," Decker went on as if he hadn't heard. "And I was counting on you to stop him. If you ask me, you're not living up to your reputation."

Dunn stood, his hands poised near his pistols. "I didn't ask you."

Decker took a sip, unconcerned. "Save your bluster for someone who scares easily. You're not about to kill me, not if you want the five thousand dollars I've promised."

"It's a promise you'd better keep," Dunn said. "I carved out the liver of the last man who tried to cheat me and fed it to the wolves."

Fargo glanced at their horses, which grazed at the far end of the clearing. In order to spirit Jess Harper out of there, he had to keep Decker's bunch busy for a minute or two, and what better way to do it than to run off their mounts. The only possible hitch was Dunn, who might be too savvy to fall for the ruse. He wormed closer, inch by silent inch, stopping when Jess lifted his head and spoke.

"Water."

Dunn turned and sneered, "What did you say, pup?"

"I'd like some water," Jess repeated. "Throat—so dry."

"Sure, I'll give you some." Dunn picked up a canteen, carried it over, and opened it under Harper's nose. "Doesn't that wet scent smell sweet?" Laughing, he poured a handful, then flung it into Jess's face. "There, pup. That should last you another day."

The lumberjacks thought the killer to be hilarious.

Fargo angled to the left to go around the camp. He never lost sight of Vic Dunn, so he noticed the instant the man snapped erect and glanced into the forest to the right of where he lay. Fargo slowly turned his head so as not to draw attention to himself. He was certain it would be Tune, and he wished he had tied her. But he was wrong.

Prima Harper crouched a dozen yards away.

Vic Dunn had already spotted the redhead. Prima realized she had been seen and started to raise her rifle, but she was no match for the professional killer. Dunn drew and fired in a blur. He would have killed her then and there had it not been for a fluke of fate. The slug hit the stock of her rifle instead of her chest, knocking the gun from her hands. She fell back, startled, which saved her from Dunn's second shot. It went high by mere inches.

Then Fargo entered the fray. He hurried his shot to save Prima and saw Dunn clutch at his head and fall. Decker dived flat behind the log but the lumberjacks shot to their feet, clawed for their hardware, and charged the trees.

Fargo had to get Prima out of there. He whipped the Colt up as he ran toward her and thumbed off two swift shots at the bullish figures converging on them. A lumberjack grabbed his chest and fell.

Prima was on her knees when Fargo reached her. He seized her arm and ran, listening to the whizzing bullets that came so close to taking their lives. To discourage the lumberjacks he snapped off a shot. Prima kept pace with him, her full cheeks flushed red from the excitement, her great mane of hair flying.

Since Fargo had no idea where she had left her mount and no time to look for it, he made straight for the Ovaro. They were halfway there when Prima cried out and stumbled. He yanked her upright and saw her favoring her left leg. "Are you hit?"

Prima nodded, wincing in pain.

The slugs were coming closer and closer as the lumberjacks took time to aim. Fargo spun, triggered two shots, then resumed their flight, bracing Prima so she wouldn't fall. Soon they were at the stallion, where Tune stood as rigid as a board, her eyes wide with fright. "What's happening?" she cried. "What is all the shooting?"

"Tell you later," Fargo said. The firing had slackened off for a moment, probably while the lumberjacks reloaded, which gave him time to grab hold of Tune and swing her into the saddle, then to give Prima a boost up behind the girl.

"What about you?" Prima asked.

"Where's your horse?"

"About a hundred yards south of here."

Fargo pointed at a hill to the northeast. "Ride there and wait. If I don't show in ten minutes, you're on your own." Both of them went to speak but he slapped the Ovaro on the rump and the stallion galloped off. Spinning, he sprinted like mad through the brush, seeking the redhead's horse. The lumberjacks started firing again but they weren't quite sure where he was and fired wide.

A handsome bay stood right where Prima had said it would be. It shied when Fargo ran up, and he had to soothe it by patting its neck and speaking softly before he could untie the reins and climb into the saddle. Decker's men were still in pursuit but they had lost sight of him and were scouring the vegetation about twenty yards off.

Fargo delayed long enough to reload the Colt. Then, raking his spurs, he bolted the bay into a gallop—toward Decker's camp instead of away from it. The lumberjacks cut loose again, only this time there were too many trees in the way. He was almost to the clearing when the unexpected occurred.

Decker suddenly materialized less than twenty feet in front of him, astride a horse. The timber king appeared taken by surprise and frantically tried to turn his mount while bringing a rifle to bear.

Fargo was going so fast that he couldn't stop, nor did he have time to shoot. In the blink of an eye they collided, the bay striking Decker's dun in the shoulder. The dun, unprepared, lost its footing and toppled, throwing Decker, but the bay kept on going. In moments Fargo swept out of the pines and reined up beside Jess Harper.

The young man groggily raised his head. His left eye was

swollen almost shut, his right black and blue. "Who—?" he said.

"Skye Fargo," Fargo said, leaping down. "We're getting you out of here." He pulled the toothpick and quickly slashed the ropes. Jess tried to stand but his circulation had been cut off for so long that his legs buckled. Fargo held him up, steered Jess to the bay, and pushed him into the saddle. Loud crunching in the brush showed the lumberjacks were flying back to the clearing and would arrive at any second.

Fargo tried to hold Jess up and mount but the young rancher kept sagging forward. A shot rang out. Then another. Pushing Jess back one more time, Fargo hooked a boot in a stirrup and managed to slide on. But Jess took up most of the saddle. He had to ride standing in the stirrups, his groin perched above the saddle horn. Trying not to think of what would happen should he slip, Fargo cut to the north and trotted into the woods.

The bay soon left the lumberjacks far to the rear. The firing tapered off but Fargo didn't slow down. He expected Decker to give chase and had to reach the women first. Once they had put a lot of distance behind them, they could relax. The timbermen couldn't track a bull buffalo if they were hanging on to its tail, and Dunn was dead.

Or was he? Fargo wondered, trying to recall if he had seen Dunn's body lying in the clearing. Soon he spied the hill and put the matter from his mind. The women were waiting near the top. Tune took one look and vaulted off the stallion.

"Jess! Oh, Jess! What have they done to you?"

The young man lifted his head and grinned weakly. "That coyote Dunn had his fun beating on me. But don't fret none. I'll be fit as a fiddle in no time."

Tune took his hand, then glanced at Fargo. "Get down. He'll ride with me."

"It would be best if I—" Fargo began, concerned she would be unable to hold Harper on if he started to fall. The girl interrupted him, stamping her foot and tugging on his leg.

"I'm not a child, darn you! Climb on down."

Prima spoke up. "Let her, Skye. She won't let anything happen to him." The redhead was pale, the left leg of her pants soaked with blood.

Against his better judgment Fargo changed horses. Prima sagged against him, her arms around his chest, her cheek pressed to his shoulder. He could feel the pressure of her full breasts on his back, and despite the circumstances there was a twitching in his loins.

"Thank you for helping me back there," Prima said in his ear, her warm breath tingling his skin.

"How bad are you hit?" Fargo asked.

"I don't know yet. I think the bleeding has stopped," Prima responded.

"Can you hold out awhile? We have to keep going," Fargo said.

"I understand. Do what you have to."

Fargo loped down the slope and off across a ribbon of a valley that petered out miles later at the base of a high bluff covered with madrones. He glanced back from time to time at Tune, who rode as if born to the saddle, one arm bent around to hold Jess on.

Another day was nearly gone. The sun hung above the horizon and the breeze had turned cooler. Fargo scouted for a spot to camp and found a site on the opposite side of the bluff, a wide shelf layered with grass and watered by a tiny spring. "We'll spend the night here," he announced. Getting off, he held up his arms and Prima eased down into them. For a moment they were body to body and the sensuous heat she gave off warmed Fargo's groin. He held back his desire and helped her to a convenient flat rock.

There was a bullet hole on the side of her pants, below the knee. Prima examined it, saying, "I wish I had a knife."

"Try mine," Fargo said, producing the toothpick with a flourish. He thought she would cut around the hole. Instead, she slit her pants from the ankle to the knee, exposing a creamy leg more finely sculpted than any Fargo had seen in a long time. The bullet had left a shallow furrow less than an inch long. Thankfully the bleeding had indeed stopped. "Looks like you'll live," Fargo said, grinning.

Prima looked him in the eyes. "I'd better. There's someone I need to repay for all he's done for me."

Fargo wanted to lean down and kiss her, but again he felt oddly uncomfortable with Tune being just a few yards away.

He turned to get his coffeepot and stopped in midstride. The youngest Britches was lavishing a kiss on Jess Harper that would have made a saloon girl blush. She caught his look as she straightened.

"What's the matter? Haven't you ever kissed anyone before?"

"Once or twice," Fargo said.

Tune took him literally. "You ought to do it more often. It's the next best thing to hot apple pie."

Prima's low laughter followed Fargo to the pinto. He held off unsaddling the horses until later, on the off chance Decker might somehow find them. Gathering wood took no time, and he had a small fire going in even less. The wood he selected gave off little smoke, which was quickly dispersed by the breeze.

Tune stopped kissing Jess long enough to fill the coffeepot at the spring. She took a seat next to Harper, clasped his hand in hers, and stared at him with adoring cow eyes. He had passed out and slept soundly.

"Shouldn't you be thinking of someone else besides him?" Fargo reminded her.

"Who?" the girl responded blankly. "There's no one else I care for as much as Jess. He's the man I'm going to marry one day."

"What about your mother and your sisters?" Fargo said.

Jarred, Tune faced Prima, who wore an enigmatic smile. "Ma! Land sakes! I'd plumb forgot about her and the others. Where are they, Miss Harper? Do you have any idea?"

Prima's smile evaporated. "I might," she said. "Before we ran from the house, we agreed to meet at the old sawmill if we were separated. Well, the girls and her went one way and Jess and I went another, and the next thing I knew, Decker's cutthroats were after us. I didn't want to lead them to the sawmill so Jess and I rode in the other direction."

"How'd Jess get caught?" Tune wanted to know.

"It was that Vic Dunn. His horse is the fastest I've ever seen." Prima gazed fondly at her son. "Jess saw that Dunn was going to catch us, so he decided to lure Dunn away from me. I wasn't going to do it but Jess told me not to worry, that he could get away if he was by himself." She shifted so her leg was nearer the fire. "He was so insistent, I rode off. But I didn't go far. I snuck back and saw they had him."

Fargo finished the account for her. "So you figured you would free him all by yourself. You're lucky I was there or you'd be dead."

"I know," Prima said softly. "But I couldn't very well leave my son in that bastard's clutches, now could I?" She saddened and sighed. "Not when he's the only son I have left."

"Mr. Fargo buried Wesley for you," Tune tactlessly declared. "He even said some words over the grave."

Prima again fixed a lingering gaze on Fargo. "So there's more to thank you for than I thought. I appreciate all you've done on our behalf."

"What will you do now? Leave Oregon Territory and go back to Arkansas?" Fargo asked.

"Never!" Prima said. "I'll rebuild, that's what I'll do. No miserable son of a bitch like Abe Decker is going to ruin me. In a year another house will be up and we'll be selling prime beef to those hungry settlers up in the Willamette Valley. In ten years we'll be very well off."

Fargo believed her. Primalia Harper had more grit than most men, and more beauty than most women. It was her beauty that occupied his thoughts over the next hour as he cleaned and bandaged her leg. She made no objection to his doing so. The whole time she simply smiled her enigmatic smile. And once, when he rested a hand on her knee, she covered his with hers and gave him a gentle squeeze.

Supper consisted of jerky and pemmican from Fargo's saddlebags. The pemmican, a mixture of lean dried meat and melted fat, he had picked up in a Nez Percé village to the north.

Since Decker hadn't shown, Fargo felt it safe to strip both animals and allowed them to graze. He gave Prima's saddle to Tune so she could prop it under Jess, then placed his over by Prima. "Your pillow for the night," he said.

Prima was chewing jerky, her rosy lips as inviting as cherry candy. "I'd like to sleep there," she said, indicating the spring. "That way I won't have to go far if I need to dress my wound in the middle of the night."

Fargo thought that highly unlikely but he did as she bid him and laid out his bedroll for her to use, saving one blanket for Tune and Jess. He sat by the fire, knees tucked to his chest, and fed small branches to the flames when needed. No one spoke for a long while. Tune had eyes only for Jess, and Prima was lost in her own thoughts.

"Will we go find Ma and my sisters in the morning?" Tune eventually broke the silence.

"If your husband is up to it," Fargo said.

The girl blushed and looked around as if for something to throw at him. "Don't be calling him that. We're not married *yet!*" she said.

"It won't be long," Fargo teased. "Any man who will buy horehound for a woman must be sweet on her."

Prima laughed again, which made Tune angrier. "I should box your ears," she huffed. "I'm not so young that I don't know when someone is poking fun at me. My sisters do it all the time and it makes me so mad I want to pound on them with an ax."

"Don't get so riled, dear," Prima said. "Mr. Fargo is just trying to help you take your mind off your problems."

"He has a strange way of doing it," Tune complained. She covered Jess with the blanket and lay down next to him, her stiff back to the fire.

"I'd say she has the right idea," Prima commented, and yawned so long and so loud it was almost as if she were pretending to be tired. Stretching, she tried to stand but her leg gave her trouble. "Care to help a lady out?"

Fargo took her arm and escorted her to the spring. After she sank down and propped herself on the saddle, he touched his hat brim and turned to leave.

"What's your hurry? I was hoping we'd talk a little while," Prima said, much louder than she needed to.

Suddenly it occurred to Fargo that she had more on her mind than conversation. The twinkle in her eyes as he sat confirmed his hunch, and he felt like a fool for not catching on sooner. "What would you care to talk about?" he asked politely.

"Anything to pass the time until Tune drifts off," Prima said softly. "I have my reputation to think of." Then, raising her voice, she declared, "It's been a long day. I might not be able to stay awake much longer."

"You've held up pretty well, considering," Fargo said, and wished he hadn't. Her lighthearted mood disappeared, her features becoming downcast.

"My Wes," Prima said, choking on the words. The tears she had held back all day streamed from her eyes and she let out a tortured sob. "My sweet, darling boy."

Fargo moved closer to comfort her, Tune be damned. His arm cradled her slender shoulders and she leaned on him, her head snuggled under his chin. Prima's whole body trembled as she wept. He let her cry herself out, and it seemed to take forever. Tune had long since fallen asleep before Prima stopped trembling and lay quietly on Fargo's chest. He figured she had fallen asleep too and went to lower her down onto the blanket. The last thing he expected was for her to tilt her head and kiss him full on the lips, yet that's exactly what she did. Her right hand found the back of his neck and gently stroked the skin. Then she drew back and sighed in contentment.

Fargo gazes into her lovely eyes. "You're a bundle of surprises."

"That's what my husband used to say all the time," Prima said wistfully. She traced the length of his jaw with a finger. "Something tells me that you're not the marrying kind, are you?"

"No," Fargo confessed.

"A rake and a rambler," Prima said, grinning. "Yet I want you anyway." Once more she rose high enough to press her luscious lips to his, her arms folding around his neck.

Fargo was ready this time. His mouth parted and his tongue glided out to meet hers halfway. She tasted delicious, like the sweetest of nectars. Their kiss lingered, warming him more than the fire ever could.

Prima wore a dreamy look when the kiss ended. "Mmm-mmm. That was nice. You're a man of vast experience, I see."

"Some," Fargo allowed.

"Don't worry, Skye," Prima said. "I won't hold it against you. You're a handsome man, and it's plain you're not a monk." She lay back, her head braced by the saddle, and touched his cheek. "You know what I want. I hope you'll be gentleman enough to oblige me and never tell a soul. And don't ask why, because I doubt you would ever understand." She paused, and her next words were uttered in a whisper. "It's been so long. I just want someone to hold me, to touch me in all the right places, to make me forget for a while."

"I do understand," Fargo told her. He started to reach for her but she stopped his hand.

"Pull the blanket over us. I wouldn't want Tune or my Jess to see, even though I suspect they've done a lot more than they let on. Every night after my Jess visits her, he walks around wearing a big grin for hours." She smiled. "Young love. It's always the best."

"I wouldn't say that." Fargo stretched out next to her and arranged the top blanket so they were covered from toes to chins. He glanced at her and she giggled in girlish glee.

"This is so silly it's funny."

"We can move somewhere else, further from the fire, if you want."

"This will do fine," Prima said, turning so they were face-to-face. "I'll just have to grit my teeth and bear the pleasure so I don't wake Tune or Jess up."

Their next kiss was more passionate. Their bodies molded together and their loins met, inflaming each of them with aroused desire. Her breasts jutted hard against his chest while his manhood did the same against her, lower down. His hands roamed to her buttocks and pressed. Her hands dawdled at his chest.

"My goodness," Prima said when they broke for air. "If you did this for a living, you'd have women lined up for miles."

The notion made Fargo grin. "I'll keep that in mind in case I ever grow tired of rambling." He lowered his lips to her neck and nibbled lightly. She shuddered as if cold, her hands locking behind his head. A fluttering gasp was her reaction when his mouth dipped to the top of the deep cleft between her breasts. He unbuttoned the upper three buttons of her flannel shirt to get at her gorgeous mounds. They sprang free, the nipples hard and erect. His tongue encircled one and he swirled it in his mouth.

Prima moaned loudly, then caught herself. Her nails raked his back and she arched her spine.

Fargo undid her shirt the rest of the way while massaging her nipples with his tongue. He placed a hand on each breast and squeezed. Prima threw back her head, her mouth forming a delightful oval, but she didn't moan or cry out. His right hand drifted across her smooth stomach to her pants, which parted as easily as the shirt. He had to tug to get them off, and in doing so the blanket slipped to one side. After covering them again, he stroked her creamy thighs.

"Oh, yes," Prima whispered. She locked her fingers in his hair and pulled his face down to her breasts again. "I like it when you lick me."

So Fargo did, lathering both mounds, while she cooed softly and squirmed in ecstasy. Some women were more sensitive in certain areas than others, and it was clear that Prima favored her breasts, especially her nipples. All he had to do was flick one with his tongue and she bucked against him, her body craving more.

At length Fargo slid a hand between her legs. Prima tensed and closed her eyes, as if she were afraid of what he would do next. Yet when his fingers touched her core, she hugged him so tightly he could hardly breathe. He slipped a finger into her tunnel, then another, and stroked. Her wet walls clung to him and she pumped her bottom to match the tempo of his strokes.

Fargo parted her legs wider and knelt between them. He had always liked long, willowy legs, and she had them in spades. Kneading her breasts with one hand, he kissed her stomach, gliding his tongue around her navel. She was panting now, trying to do it quietly but failing, lost in sexual joy. He touched the tip of his pole to her slit, thinking he would enter her slowly, but she had other ideas. Her bottom leaped at him, impaling him in her silken sheath, before he quite knew what had happened.

"Now," Prima urged. "I'm so close."

Although he would rather have prolonged their lovemaking, Fargo complied, rocking his hips and thrusting into her so hard he lifted her off the ground. She clung to him, lavishing tiny kisses on his chest and neck, her nails gouging his shoulders. How long they pumped, he couldn't say, but eventually he felt a contraction deep within her and at that very moment she bit down on his arm to keep from crying out.

Fargo let himself go, ramming into her again and again, rushing his own release. When the explosion came, he thought the world would end. He coasted to a stop and lay on her heaving chest, listening to her heart beat wildly. Lethargy crept over him, and he let himself start to drift off. In another few seconds he would have been sound asleep, but suddenly a finger tapped him on the back.

"I'm sorry to bother you," Tune Britches said, "but I think someone is riding this way."

12

Prima shot up so fast that Fargo fell off her and had to scramble to keep the blanket over them. She hurried buttoning her shirt while he glanced at Tune, wondering how much she had seen. He half suspected that she was playing some sort of game, but her worried expression showed differently. He sat up, listening, and heard a faint crackle of underbrush. "Put out the fire," he ordered.

Tune ran to obey, and Fargo pulled his pants up. Prima was wriggling into hers. She paused to grab his arm. "Do you think it could be Decker?"

"I can't see him stumbling around in the dark looking for us," Fargo said, "but maybe he's smarter than I give him credit for being. Maybe he guessed we wouldn't go very far with Jess in the shape he's in." Strapping on his gunbelt, he slid out from under the blanket and stood. As he claimed his hat he heard the crackling again, only closer. The sound came from the east.

The flames were dying out. Tune had poured the coffee on them to get the job done, but in so doing she created a thick column of smoke that could be seen from a long ways off.

Fargo grabbed his saddle and saddle blanket and hastened to the Ovaro. He soon had both horses ready to go and was lashing his bedroll behind the cantle when the night was rent by a shout. He didn't catch the words but he recognized the voice: Rand's.

Prima had dressed and was helping Tune guide Jess to their mounts. The young man acted sluggish, his face as swollen as ever. "I'm sorry to be such a bother," he said over and over through puffy, cracked lips.

Fargo boosted Jess onto the bay and Tune clambered up.

The smoke had dwindled, but too late. From the other side of the bluff rumbled the beat of heavy hooves. He forked the Ovaro, helped Prima climb on, and headed down the slope as rapidly as was safe.

"They must want us awful badly," Prima remarked.

"Decker won't want to leave any witnesses," Fargo said. "He has to kill all of us or make himself scarce in these parts, and he's not about to close down his sawmill."

"I was hoping he'd give up after losing Dunn," Prima said. "But maybe it's just made him more desperate than ever."

Riding under a moonless sky was a tricky proposition. Fargo picked his way with care, well aware that a log, a rut, a cleft, an animal burrow, all could cripple a horse. Losing an animal then would mean they had to make a stand, and he had no illusions about the outcome. In the dark he couldn't protect the women and Jess and put up a good fight at the same time.

They had put no more than half a mile behind them when two gunshots echoed across the valley, followed seconds later by two more.

"A signal, you think?" Prima said.

"One of them found the fire," Fargo guessed. But he still felt confident he would elude them. After all, they couldn't track at night.

"Look," Prima said minutes later.

Twisting, Fargo spied a small circle of light on the bluff. It flared briefly, then moved slowly down the slope. "A torch," he said. "They'll go faster now. And so will we."

Suiting his actions to his words, Fargo trotted along the valley floor, shying away from patches of timber and heavy brush. Speed was all that mattered, speed and one more thing. "I think I've earned the right to learn the truth about this feud, don't you?" He waited, but she made no reply. "From what I've heard, Decker wants to marry one of the Britches but she doesn't want anything to do with him. Is that what this is all about?"

"I promised Maude I wouldn't say anything, remember?" Prima reminded him.

"You'd rather I risk my life and not know why?" Fargo shot back. "Is that fair?"

"No, it's not," Prima said softly. She fell silent for a little bit. "Very well. It can't hurt, and Maude will just have to accept it or find herself a new friend." Prima paused. "About a year ago Decker took a shine to one of the Britches girls. He fell for her hard, and courted her for the longest time. Everyone was talking about it, wondering what he saw in her."

The statement puzzled Fargo but he didn't interrupt. At last he was on the verge of discovering the real reason behind all the bloodshed.

"Abe Decker took it for granted she would be his wife. Yet when he proposed, she flatly turned him down and threatened to have nothing more to do with him if he ever brought the subject up again," Prima related.

"A man like Decker wouldn't take that very well," Fargo mentioned.

"He didn't. Oh, for a while he went along with her, but then he decided she was going to be his whether she liked the idea or not. They had terrible arguments. They threw things at one another and yelled and cursed, once right at the trading post. Folks began to poke fun at Decker behind his back. One lumberjack laughed at him to his face and Decker beat the man within an inch of his life."

"But if he loves one of them so much," Fargo said, "why is he trying to kill them?"

"I'm getting to that," Prima answered. "About eight weeks ago he ran into the family on the trail to the post. He proposed again but she said no. It made him so mad he hit her right in front of the others."

"And?" Fargo prompted when she stopped.

"Sym, Melody, and Harmony all tore into him. Sym clubbed him with her rifle, and when he fell they closed in and kicked him half to death. By the time they were done, Decker looked a lot like my Jess looks now."

"Did Leland and Maude join in?" Fargo asked.

"No. Leland just sat on the wagon, laughing. Maude tried to stop it but she never has been able to control her brood. Little Tune wasn't there. She was off with Jess."

So now Fargo knew, and knowing, he almost regretted getting involved. "Shortly after the beating Decker sent for Vic Dunn?"

"Not right away, not until the girls started bragging and

spreading the story. I think that's what drove Decker over the edge. He's a proud man, and his pride was hurt. Plus he was in love, and she rejected him. Men have killed for lots less."

Fargo nodded. "Which one was it?" He suspected Melody since she was the one who had tried to bushwhack Decker.

"I'm sorry, I can't say. I've broken my promise as it is." Prima placed a hand on his shoulder. "Does it really matter, anyway? We can't let Decker kill them, even if they partly do deserve it."

"No, we can't," Fargo said, without much conviction.

"I admit the girls brought it on themselves," Prima elaborated. "They always have been too wild for their own damn good. Maude should have sent them off somewhere for proper schooling so they'd learn to behave like ladies instead of hellcats."

For the next hour Fargo pressed on deep into the rolling mountains. He was hoping Decker would give up once the torch went out, but when it did they lit another. Slowly but surely Decker narrowed the distance. Fargo figured the timbermen would overtake him before dawn unless he came up with an idea to shake them.

A ridge appeared on the left and Fargo reined the Ovaro in that direction. A deadfall along the bottom forced him to detour wide, so by the time he reached the top the torch was only a few hundred yards off and he could distinguish vague outlines of the riders. Reining up, he slid off, grabbed the Sharps, and walked a few yards off.

"What are you doing?" Tune asked. "Why did we stop? You're not thinking of fighting them, are you?"

"Not here, but I will have to sooner or later," Fargo replied. Sinking to one knee, he wedged the rifle stock to his shoulder. "For now I just want to slow them down." He tried to get a bead on one of the vague shapes but Decker's killers were in heavy timber and trees kept spoiling his aim. It would be sheer luck if he hit one of them. He focused on the torch, then lowered the sights to a bulky shape underneath it, and fired. Without waiting to see the result, he worked the lever that lowered the breechblock, inserted another cartridge, and fired again.

An average man could fire a Sharps about four times in sixty seconds. Fargo was much more skilled than average, and over the next minute he squeezed off six shots, right into the middle of the knot of pursuers.

At the first booming retort, the torch waved wildly. There were strident yells. After the second shot the torch seemed to fly southward but didn't go far; either the rider ran into a low limb and was unhorsed or he dropped it, because it fluttered to the ground, sputtered a little, and slowly went out. Decker and his men returned fire, but wildly. They had no idea where Fargo was and shot at shadows.

Grinning, Fargo ran to the Ovaro and mounted. It would take Decker a while to figure out the ruse and decide it was safe to go on, and by then Fargo hoped to gain enough of a lead to lose him. Fargo walked the horses for over a hundred yards so as not to make noise that would give them away, then he quickly brought the Ovaro to a lope. Tune stayed close to the pinto's left flank.

An hour later Fargo stopped again, this time high on a treeless spine that afforded a panoramic view of the countryside. He looked and looked but saw no sign of another torch. "I think we shook them," he announced, and faced Prima. "Can you find your way to that old sawmill on Darby Creek from here?"

"I don't know," Prima answered. "I'm not sure of where we are."

"I can," Tune declared. "My sisters and me have been all over this territory. I could find it blindfolded."

"By morning?" Fargo asked.

"Heck, before sunrise we'll be there."

And she was as good as her word. The eastern sky had paled to pink but the sun had not yet appeared when they rode over the crest of a hill and saw a huge structure below them, darkened by the shadow of an adjacent mountain. "That's it," Tune said. "But I don't see any sign of my ma or the others."

Jess Harper, who had rarely uttered a word all night, licked his lips and said, "They wouldn't leave their horses right out in plain sight, you silly goose."

"No, I guess they wouldn't," Tune said. She smiled sweetly at him and puckered her lips as if to kiss him. "You're so smart. It does a woman proud to know her man can use his head."

Jess beamed and puffed up his chest.

"Young love," Prima whispered happily to Skye. "Isn't it wonderful?"

Fargo rolled his eyes upward and rode on. A game trail brought them to the edge of a grassy tract which bordered the old mill. Fargo halted under the oaks and alighted. "All of you wait here," he cautioned, drawing the Colt.

"What for?" Tune asked. "I want to see my ma."

"I'll make sure no one else is there," Fargo said.

"Who else would be? Decker is miles away. I want to go now," Tune said, pouting, and lifted her reins to do just that.

Prima held up a hand. "Listen to Mr. Fargo, Tuney Britches. We can't be taking needless risks. For all we know, Decker gave up chasing us and came here, figuring this was the only place around where anyone could lay low awhile."

Fargo left before the girl could object, gliding along the tree line until he stood in the cool shadow of the huge building. From a distance the sawmill had seemed solid and well kept, as if it had been built the day before. But up close the rotting timbers and cobwebs were apparent, as were wide cracks in the walls themselves. Some of the supports had split, and Fargo reckoned it wouldn't be too many years before the whole place came tumbling down like a house of cards.

Moving soundlessly to the nearest corner, Fargo cocked an ear and listened. The wind whispered against the mill. Above him a pair of sparrows took wing. He heard no voices, nor was there any other evidence the Britches were inside. Possibly they had heard the horses and feared it was Decker, he mused. Ahead loomed a doorway, the door hanging by a single hinge, the black interior of the mill seeming to gape at him like the maw of a ravenous grizzly.

Fargo warily approached the doorway and placed his back to the jamb. Crouching, he braced his legs, then shot inside, angling to the right and rolling on one shoulder. He came up with the Colt cocked and leveled but his precaution had been wasted. There was no gunfire. Shafts of sunlight streaming through windows and holes in the ceiling revealed a large room, empty except for a few rotting workbenches and the framework for a massive saw. Dust covered everything, and thanks to the dust Fargo discovered he wasn't alone.

A recent trail of tracks led from the entrance to a closed door on the other side. There were more tracks about the room, made at random. Most were small, convincing Fargo they had been made by women. One set was larger than the rest. Sym's, he reasoned.

Fargo moved stealthily across to the door. Knowing how quick on the trigger the Britches were, he didn't throw it open. Again he stood to one side, then rapped lightly. "Maude? It's Fargo. Are you in there?"

A few seconds of quiet ensued, and Fargo wondered if the family had gone elsewhere, perhaps searching for Tune and the Harpers.

"Come on in, Mr. Fargo," Maude called out, a peculiar note in her voice, as if she were greatly relieved or a bit scared.

Working the wooden latch, Fargo stepped into the next room, a greeting on his lips. The greeting died when a hard object gouged into his right temple and a man addressed him.

"Freeze, mister, unless you want your brains scattered from here to hell and back."

Fargo did as he was told. Playing the hero would only get him killed, while playing along might give him a chance to turn the tables. A dirty hand plucked the Colt from his fingers and he was shoved forward so roughly he nearly tripped over his own feet. Turning, he confronted a wiry, ratty man whose face sparkled with animal glee.

"Well, lookee here. I caught me the high-and-mighty Skye Fargo," the man said, snickering. "And Dunn claimed you were a tough one. You don't look so tough to me."

The Britches were all there, Maude by the left-hand wall, her daughters seated on rickety chairs at a dusty table that had one leg missing. An empty crate had been used to prop it up. Melody still had her shoulder bandaged, Harmony now had her side bandaged, while Sym simply looked as mean as ever.

"Wait until the boss sees you," the lumberjack had gone on. "He'll give me a bonus." Shoving Fargo's Colt under his belt, he leaned against the wall and smirked. "The name is Garvey, in case you're wondering. I work for Mr. Decker. He's smart as a fox, that man."

"If you say so," Fargo said. He saw the hilt of a big knife sticking above the top of the man's left boot.

"Oh, I know so, mister," Garvey said. "When he attacked the Harper place, he had me stay in the trees and keep watch in case any of the pesky Britches slipped past him. I saw the ladies ride off and followed them here."

"You didn't take them back to Decker?" Fargo asked, to keep the man talking and give himself time to think.

"I was going to," Garvey said, "until these lovely ladies let it slip that they were to meet Prima Harper here."

Sym half rose from her chair. "Let it slip, hell! The damned runt used Ma for target practice. He threatened to put a bullet in her gut if we didn't tell him why we came straight here from the Harpers'."

Garvey chuckled. "A man does what he has to, missy. You're just mad because I got the drop on you."

"Put down that gun and I'll show you how much of a man you are," Sym growled. "Why, I'm more man than you'll ever be."

"I wouldn't doubt that for a minute," Garvey said. "But I don't aim to be stomped half to death like Abe, so I'll hold on to my hardware, if you don't mind." He rubbed the stubble on his chin and thought out loud. "Now that I've got all of you, what should I do? I've never killed a woman before and I don't intend to start, so I'll have to take you ladies to the boss." Garvey extended his arm toward Fargo. "But you, now. Killing you will be a pleasure. You shot my good friend Petey."

Maude came to Fargo's defense. "Decker might want him alive, Mr. Garvey. You should take him along too."

"Begging your pardon, ma'am," Garvey said, "but Decker made it clear he wants Fargo dead in the worst way. Fargo tricked him, you see, made Decker think he was Dunn. And the boss can't stand for anyone to make a fool of him."

"We know," Maude said, "all too well."

"Enough said, then." Garvey sighted down the barrel, aiming low, below Fargo's belt. "I think you should die real slow. I want to hear you scream a little."

Fargo tensed to spring. While the lumberjack talked, he had edged a few inches closer. Not enough for him to reach Garvey in a single jump, but it would have to do.

The ratty man grinned wickedly. He steadied his arm, about

to fire, when from the other room came a high-pitched wail that caused him to hesitate and swivel his head toward the doorway.

"Ma! Ma! Where are you?"

It was the opening Fargo needed, the only one he was likely to get. He took two bounds and leaped, his arms flung out. The Colt banged but Garvey had moved his hand, not much but enough to send the slug into the floor instead of Fargo. Then Fargo tackled him. Fargo locked his fingers on the smaller man's gun arm and smashed Garvey's wrist on the floor, again and again. At the third blow Garvey let go of the gun. Twisting like a snake, he rammed a heavy boot into Fargo's midsection, knocking Fargo to one side. It enabled Garvey to regain his feet, and when he uncurled he had the big butcher knife in his skinny hand.

Fargo rose, holding the toothpick. He parried a blow that would have made a gelding of him and delivered one that was neatly blocked. The little man knew how to wield a knife, how to thrust, counter, and slash far better than Terrell had.

Feinting, Fargo drove his blade at the other's thigh, but he was easily evaded. However, as Garvey darted aside, a chair flew out of the air and caught him on the shoulder. Garvey stumbled forward, right into the toothpick. It was hard to say who was more surprised. Fargo felt his hand grow sticky and drew it back to finish the lumberjack off, but another blow wasn't needed.

Garvey looked down at himself, then over his shoulder. Sym was a few feet away, sneering in sadistic delight. "Well, I'll be damned," he said. "That she-cat got me after all." With that, he died, falling where he stood, the butcher knife clattering beside him.

Sym reached for another chair. "Now it's your turn!" she bellowed at Fargo, whipping it overhead. "This is for laying a hand on me." She bunched her broad shoulders to throw it.

"No!" Maude yelled, dashing between them. "Put that down this instant, Symphony Britches. You're not to touch Mr. Fargo. He's on our side."

"He hurt me!" Sym balked. "I won't let anyone do that to me and get away with it."

Maude held her ground, her mousey frame dwarfed by her bullish daughter. "Do as I say. So long as you're part of this family, you'll listen when you're told what to do." She gestured at the chair. "Now, young lady."

Sym tossed the chair against the wall with such force it shattered. Fists clenched, she stalked out, nearly plowing Tuney over when the smaller girl appeared in the doorway. Tuney jumped out of her older sister's path, spotted her mother, and, with a squeal of joy, ran to Maude.

Mother and youngest embraced, and for the moment Fargo was forgotten. He found his Colt and walked over to the table. "I have some bad news to pass on," he announced, and caught Maude's eye.

Briefly Fargo told them of Leland's death. Harmony and Melody burst into tears. Maude closed her eyes and appeared to age five years in five seconds. "I feared as much," she said. "I knew something was dreadfully wrong. I could feel it in my bones."

"Abe Decker will pay!" Melody vowed, dabbing at her eyes. "We won't rest until he's worm food."

"You tried once already," Fargo reminded her, feeling little sympathy since he blamed her for all the violence. Or was she to blame? he wondered. "All these lives lost because Decker fell in love with you," he commented to sound her out. "It would have been better for everyone if the two of you had hated one another from the start."

"Me?" Melody blurted, shocked.

"Her?" Harmony added, and stopped crying. "Where'd you ever get such a crazy idea? Melody wouldn't let that ape within fifty feet of her. She has better taste than that."

"Then it was you," Fargo told the blonde. "That hot-blooded nature of yours got you into more trouble than you bargained for."

Whatever reply was on Harmony's lips died when footsteps pounded in the other room. Fargo whirled and drew the Colt. A shadow filled the doorway moments before the person did. It was Prima Harper.

"Prima, dear," Maude said. "I'm so glad you escaped too. Now we can sit down and plan our next step. With Mr. Fargo to help us, we at least have a prayer."

"Not if we don't get out of this place," Prima said. "Grab your things and let's go before it's too late." She motioned over a shoulder. "Decker and his men are coming down the mountain to the north. They'll be here any second."

13

Fargo joined the rush from the sawmill. Jess Harper waited outside, on the bay, holding the reins to the Ovaro. "I'll take those," Fargo said while surveying the mountain Prima had mentioned. At first he saw no one, just firs and spruce and boulders. Then movement on the lower slope revealed three riders he figured were Decker, Rand, and Brickman.

"Our horses are around back," Maude said, and took a few steps. Suddenly she halted. "Wait a minute! Where's Sym? She came out here, didn't she?"

Jess answered. "Yes, ma'am. I saw her stomp around the corner a couple of minutes ago. She looked mad enough to spit nails."

"Sym has always been a little temperamental," Maude commented, going on.

Fargo mounted and trailed them. Temperamental wasn't the word he'd use to describe Symphony Britches. "Vicious" was more like it. She was as tough as any man he'd ever met and more dangerous than most. And he didn't like to think of her lurking out there somewhere, maybe with a rifle in hand, waiting for a chance to pick him off.

Three horses grazed behind the mill. Harmony and Melody ran to fetch them while Maude wrung her hands in worry. "Sym's not here! Lord, I hope she doesn't run into Decker. There's no telling what he'd do to her."

Fargo had reined up at the corner so he could keep an eye on the front of the building. He pulled the Sharps out and fed in a cartridge. Should he go with them? he asked himself. Or should he make a stand there at the mill to give the women and the boy time to get away? The odds were only three to one and the timbermen lacked his experience. He could end it, right there, and he said as much.

"You want us to go off by ourselves?" Maude said uncertainly. "I don't know if I like that notion. Without Sym, we'd be easy pickings."

"Only if they get past me, which they won't," Fargo assured her. He felt Prima's eyes on him and twisted. "I won't be long. Keep a rein on the others until I catch up."

"Be careful, Skye Fargo," the redhead said. "I wouldn't want anything to happen to you." Her comment drew a surprised look from Maude, and she added, "Not after all you've done on our behalf. You're the only true friend we have."

Prima wound up riding double with her son. Tune, annoyed at the switch, had to ride with Melody. Maude waved as they trotted into the forest and cut to the southeast.

Fargo was glad to see them go. By himself he could carry the fight to Decker instead of always being on the defensive. He rode to within a few yards of the front corner and climbed down.

Decker and his henchmen were off the mountain and riding along the tree line on the west side of the valley. They all held rifles and were hugging the shadows as much as possible. Apparently they had no idea they had been spotted.

Bracing the Sharps against the corner, Fargo elevated the rear sight and adjusted it for the range. He aimed at Abe Decker. Once the timber lord was dead, the Britches would be safe. Decker was the cause of all the bloodshed. Without him to hire men like Dunn and spur his own men to violence, the feud would end. He settled the front bead on the center of Decker's chest and aligned the bead with the rear sight. Just before firing he held his breath to steady his arms and shoulder. Finally, believing he had a perfect shot, he stroked the trigger.

Even as Fargo did, Decker came to a low limb and ducked under it. The bullet meant for his chest hit his hat instead and sent it sailing. As the blast rolled across the valley, Decker dived from his mount and the others followed suit.

Fargo reloaded quickly but it was too late for another shot. Once again mere chance had foiled him. The timbermen now had a fair idea where he was and would lose no time converging. He stepped to the Ovaro and led it into the brush a dozen yards, where the growth would screen it from prying eyes. Returning to the mill, he jogged to the rear corner, peeked out to be sure none of the timbermen had appeared, then sprinted to the next corner and crouched.

Removing his hat, Fargo put his eye to the edge. The high grass rippled in the wind. The trees rustled and swayed. He saw a swallow cavorting above the grass and a jay off in the pines. He watched the jay, having learned a trick or two from the Indians. A minute went by and the bird sat on the limb, looking about and uttering its harsh *shack-shack-shack* call every so often. Just when Fargo thought he had erred and the timbermen were all at the other end of the mill, the jay gave a start and flapped frantically into the sky, circling once to screech at something in the trees below.

Fargo raised the Sharps and waited. The swallow was next to take startled flight, swooping off in great circles. Fargo concentrated on the area under the first circle the swallow made and saw the top of the grass sway as if pushed by an object sliding along the ground. Easing onto his stomach, he pointed the rifle at the moving grass.

In due course a large shape became visible. A hand slid into sight, pushing against the grass, and a moment later a head poked out. It was Rand, and he saw Fargo.

Fargo fired as the lumberjack rolled to the left. The grass closed around Rand, giving Fargo no idea whether his shot had been accurate or not. Placing his hat back on, he slid into the grass to his left and circled around to come up on the big lumberjack from behind. He had covered about half the distance when he heard soft rustling directly ahead.

Rand had the same idea and was coming straight toward him.

Moving silently, Fargo crawled to the left a few feet. He bent the grass surrounding him so that he was completely hidden. Then he drew his Colt.

A dozen yards off grass parted and Rand appeared for the second time. He looked toward the mill. The grin he wore showed he thought he was being as slick as hot grease.

Fargo slowly extended the Colt. He had already taken the precaution of thumbing back the hammer so Rand wouldn't hear the click. The lumberjack came within a foot of his hiding place but failed to notice him. Fargo could easily squeeze the trigger and Rand would never know what happened. But that would have been too easy.

"Rand," Fargo said softly.

The lumberjack was fast for his size. He twisted and pushed to one knee while swinging his rifle around. The gun was almost level when Fargo fired, the slug taking Rand high in the chest and flipping him onto his back. Rand dropped the rifle as he fell. Wheezing, he propped an elbow under him and rose partway, his other hand creeping toward the Colt at his waist. "Damn you," he snarled. "I'll see you in hell!"

"Never make a threat you can't keep," Fargo said, and shot the man again, between the eyes. Rising, he swiftly replaced the spent cartridges, then grabbed the Sharps and made for the rear of the sawmill.

To the east a rifle cracked. Fargo heard the slug tear into the ground almost at his feet. He flattened, snaked to the left, then froze. Whoever was out there would shoot at the least little movement. He would be smarter waiting out the shooter. Resting his chin on his forearm, he listened for any indication that Decker or Brickman was trying to sneak up on him.

From somewhere in the mill came a loud thump. Fargo was pleased to hear it since it confirmed one of his enemies was inside and no immediate threat. Or so he thought until a scraping noise drew his gaze to a fractured window twelve feet up on the back wall and there knelt Decker, taking aim.

Fargo flipped to the side just as the rifle spat smoke and lead. The slug smacked into the earth so close to his ear that bits of dirt sprayed onto his skin. He leaped to his feet and snapped off a shot with the Sharps that missed. Almost instantly Brickman opened up from the forest to the east.

Caught in the open, Fargo didn't have a chance. He had to reach cover. So, drawing the Colt, he banged a shot at each of them and dashed madly for the southwest corner. Another slug plowed into the decaying wood as he ducked around the building. Since they had his position pegged, Fargo kept running until he reached a door cracked open several inches. He pushed, and winced as the hinges creaked loud enough to raise the dead. Ducking inside, he moved to the right, to a stack of planks layered thick with dust. Behind these he crouched to catch his breath and plot his next move.

Fargo regretted having come inside. By now Brickman was probably covering the door he had entered. Unwittingly, he had boxed himself in, unless he could slip past Decker. He reloaded the rifle and the pistol, then stalked among the scattered debris, bent low so no one would spot him.

Someone did, though. Fargo was going past a huge roll of rusted wire when a rifle cracked from the outside doorway. The roll jumped as if alive, and Fargo hugged the floor. He wriggled to a spot where he could see the door, but no one was there.

Fargo glanced toward the rear of the room where a smaller door led to another part of the mill. Back there somewhere was Decker. His best avenue of escape lay in going to the front of the sawmill, through the same rooms he had passed through earlier.

Taking advantage of the cover available, Fargo crawled to a narrow hallway filled with cobwebs. He rose into a crouch and entered, keeping his back to the wall so he could see both ways. Silken, clinging cobwebs stuck to him like glue. He ducked under one only to run smack into another that covered the lower half of his face. Jerking aside, he tried to pull loose but the cobweb clung fast. He reached up to brush it off and felt something crawling on his cheek. The next moment a large spider clambered onto the tip of his nose. In the dim light from the room he could see its bulging black abdomen and a trace of red color on its underside. He didn't need to flip it over to see the rest of the red hourglass marking. He knew it was a black widow.

Fargo held still. A bite from a black widow sometimes proved fatal. In instances where it didn't, the people bitten became so sick they were laid up for weeks or months on end. The spider moved slowly up the bridge of his nose and stopped halfway to his eyes. He wanted to brush it off but was afraid any movement would cause it to strike.

From the room Fargo had vacated a low voice called out. "Boss, is that you?"

"Of course it's me, you jackass. Yell a little louder so Fargo will know where we are too."

"Where is he, boss? I lost him."

"So did I, but he can't have gone far. Search for him."

Fargo couldn't stay there any longer. It was only a matter of seconds before one of them thought to look into the hallway. He slowly raised his right hand until his fingers were inches from his nose. The black widow seemed fascinated by his eyes and was edging toward them. Hardly breathing, he tucked the nail of his index finger against his thumb, tensed his hand, and lowered his fingers as close to the black widow as he dared without touching it.

The spider somehow sensed the threat and turned toward his hand. Fargo flicked his nail. It hit the black widow in the head and catapulted it into the dark.

Rising, Fargo ran. He plowed through other webs and swatted at anything that resembled a spider. A closed door appeared. There was a latch, and Fargo grasped it and lifted, but the latch refused to budge.

"I found him, boss! Down here!"

The boom of a rifle reverberated in the confines of the hall. A bullet smashed into the closed door, giving Fargo the idea to draw his Colt and fire twice at the latch. Throwing his shoulder against the boards, he slammed the door open and tumbled to the floor beyond.

A body lay a few yards away. It was Garvey, as white as flour, as stiff as a broom handle. Fargo vaulted over the man and out the other door as boots pounded in the hallway. Now all he had to do was cross the huge chamber to the entrance. He ran hard, then drew up short. Another black widow was crawling up his leg and had nearly reached his groin. The sight brought goose bumps to his flesh, and he bent to flick it off as he had the first one. But as he went to do so, the spider did an amazing feat; it jumped onto the back of his hand.

Fargo turned to stone and listened to the drum of boots growing nearer and nearer while the black widow crawled toward his wrist. He had to time his move just right. The moment the spider crawled off his skin onto the sleeve of his buckskin he whipped his arm and flung the spider against the side of a partially completed cabinet. It hit with a soft splat. Taking several rapid strides, Fargo reached the side of the cabinet and hunkered down as a bulky figure filled the doorway.

Brickman entered, trailed by his employer. "He's gone, boss. He must have made it out."

Abe Decker swung his rifle from side to side. "Maybe. Maybe he's still here, waiting to ambush us. Keep low and look."

Fargo slipped the Colt from its holster. He had a clear shot at Brickman but not Decker, and since he would rather kill the timber king than the underling, he held his fire. Brickman went to the right, Decker to the left. Fargo eased to the back of the cabinet and saw Decker moving past a workbench. He took deliberate aim. This time there would be no mistakes. There were no low limbs. No fluke would spare Abe Decker's life.

All Fargo had to do was cock the pistol. He touched his thumb to the hammer and pulled back slowly to mute the noise. Behind him boots crashed, and before he could whirl, the cabinet crashed down on top of him, pinning his legs.

Brickman loomed above him. He had Fargo dead to rights, and he cackled as he aimed and squeezed the trigger.

Fargo had a split second's forewarning. He wrenched his body to the left as the rifle went off and the bullet tore into the floor instead of his head. The lumberjack went to shoot again but Fargo fired first, fanning the Colt three times. Fanning was no good for shooting at a distance, but at close range it got the job done admirably well. His three shots hit Brickman in the sternum and rocked him on his heels, yet somehow Brickman kept his feet and tried to raise his rifle. Fargo shot him in the head.

Decker brought his rifle into play from the shelter of the workbench, his lead clipping splinters off the cabinet.

Fargo had one shot left in the Colt. He used it to make Decker drop from sight, then he strained against the heavy cabinet and moved it enough to slide his legs out from under. His left ankle ached badly, slowing him as he scrambled to his feet and limped off seeking other cover. Lethal hornets nipped at his heels every step of the way.

The frame for the giant saw was the nearest sanctuary. Fargo darted behind it and forked five cartridges from his gunbelt. Decker had stopped firing and Fargo assumed the timberman was moving to a better vantage point. He replaced the last cartridge, swiveled, and rose high enough to see over the frame.

The room was quiet and empty save for the dust sparkling in the air. Brickman lay on his back, blank eyes fixed on the ceiling. Of Decker there was no sign, but Fargo wasn't fooled. The man had to be there. He wormed along the bottom of the frame to where he could see most of the room clearly, but still no Decker.

Fargo waited with the patience of the Sioux Indians among whom he had once lived for the timber king to move or make a sound. Only someone wilderness-bred could stay completely still for long minutes on end, a fact Indians often exploited when fighting whites. Most warriors knew that if they waited long enough, their white foes would give themselves away.

So Fargo was mildly surprised when several minutes went by and the only noise in the enormous room was the buzzing of a fly. Then, from somewhere to the east, came the patter of hooves. Fargo leaped up and ran out into the brilliant sunlight. He blinked in the harsh glare, raised a hand over his eyes, and spotted Decker in full flight to the south. Bringing the Sharps up, Fargo lowered his cheek to the stock to aim but Decker reached the forest and in moments was gone.

"Damn it," Fargo grumbled. Now he would have to track Decker down, which might take the rest of the day, or more. And he'd had his heart set on finally ending the feud. Disappointed, he shifted the rifle to his side and turned to go fetch the Ovaro.

From out of nowhere whizzed a long metal bar. Fargo saw it sweeping toward his head and tried to throw himself out of the way. He managed to avoid having his skull bashed in but the bar still clipped him solidly on the temple and dropped him in his tracks. Flooded by pain, Fargo was vaguely aware of a shadowy shape towering over him and of having the rifle taken from his limp fingers. He heard rather than felt the Colt being snatched from its holster.

"There now. We can do this right."

Slowly Fargo's vision cleared and he could see the big woman glaring down at him. He tried to stand but the bar struck his hand, lancing his arm with torment.

"You'll move when I tell you to move, bastard, and not be-

144

fore," Symphony Britches dictated. She poked him in the ribs and snickered. "I aim to have me some fun with you before I do what I should have done the first time I laid eyes on you."

"But we're on the same side," Fargo responded, trying to appeal to her better nature. He couldn't believe she continued to hold a hateful grudge after all he had done for her family.

"I'm on my own side, and it's the only one that matters to me," Sym said, stepping back.

"What about your family? Don't they count?" Fargo asked. He schemed to stall her until his head and hand stopped hurting enough for him to be able to jump her.

"Oh, they count some," Sym said. She tapped one hand with the end of the rusted bar. "But they don't tell me what to do. Not even Ma can boss me when I don't want to be bossed. I'll live my life any way I see fit, and that's that."

"You don't care that Decker got away? That he's probably hunting them down right this minute?"

Sym shook her head. "I ain't worried. Abe couldn't track one of them there elephants if he was two feet behind it." She chuckled with gusto. "The man is as helpless in the woods as a newborn babe."

"Even he can track that many horses," Fargo said.

"Not Abe," Sym insisted. "You just don't know him like I do." She seemed to relax a little and gazed rather regretfully off at the mountains. "Beats me what I ever saw in that worthless trash. I should have put him in his place the first time he asked to court me."

So astounded was Fargo by the news that he could only gape. "*You* were the one, all along? You're the one Decker wanted to marry?"

"What's so strange about that?" Sym said curtly. "I'm a woman, ain't I? As much or more of a woman than Melody and Harmony combined. I can make any man just as happy as they can. Hell, I can do it better."

"Decker and you," Fargo said softly, unable to shake his amazement. It would never have occurred to him in a thousand years that Sym was the one Decker fancied.

"I'd be Mrs. Decker now if the idiot had his way," Sym said in disgust. "Imagine that! Me, taking up an apron and raising a bunch of sprouts for a man who isn't but half as strong as I am. We'd be the laughingstock of the territory once word got out."

"You made Decker a laughingstock," Fargo reminded her, and was brutally hit on the knee for his observation. Gripping his leg with both hands, he curled into a ball and fought off the splitting torment. She had nearly shattered the kneecap.

"He asked for it!" Sym hissed. "He laid a hand on me. And no one does that without paying a price, as you're learning the hard way." She kicked Fargo in the thigh. "Too bad about you, though, little man. I was taking a shine to your handsome face when you went and beat on me. If you hadn't, you and me might have enjoyed a tumble or two in the hay."

Fargo knew he shouldn't respond, knew he shouldn't do anything to make her madder, but he couldn't help himself. "I'd rather be gelded."

Sym's face contorted. "Why, you—" she said, and couldn't think of words vile enough to do him justice. Drawing back the bar, she announced, "I'm going to bust you to bits. And you want to know something? I'll enjoy every second."

"Enjoy this," Fargo said. He lashed out with his good leg, catching her in the knee with his boot heel. She cried out and staggered, then lifted the bar higher and drove it at his neck. Fargo rolled and felt air fan his cheek. He heaved into a crouch and brought his arm up in time to block a sideways blow that would have ruptured his ear. His forearms took the brunt, pain shooting clear to his shoulders.

"Damn you, mister," Sym said, circling, favoring her one leg. "You just won't learn, will you? After I'm done beating on you, I'll hang you upside down from a beam and leave you here to rot."

Fargo saw her tense and leaped out of the way of the lunge. Shifting, he landed a punch to her ribs that made her wince and almost knocked her down. Hellion that she was, she swung low, planting the bar on his shin. It hurt, but not enough to drop him. Fargo skipped to the right, seeking an opening. He expected her to swing again. Instead, she caught him off guard by suddenly hurling the bar at his groin. Only his lightning reflexes spared his manhood, but the jolt he took on his inner thigh crumpled him to the ground and before he could

146

rise she stood over him once again with the bar poised to strike.

"Got any last words, you miserable son of a bitch?" Sym Britches said, and struck.

14

Skye Fargo saw the thick bar streaking toward his face and thought his time had come. He couldn't move out of the way quickly enough, couldn't raise his arms in time to protect himself.

Then Sym did a strange thing. She flew backward as if trying to take flight, her arms flapping wildly, a look of total shock on her fleshy features. The bar left her fingers as she slammed to the ground and slid a few feet.

A full second later the shot sounded, rippling down across the valley from the mountain slope to the west and bouncing off the slope to the east. Fargo heard it twice, as it were. Rolling onto his stomach, he crawled briskly to the Sharps and the Colt, then into the grass. From where he lay he could see Sym's features, peaceful in death, and the gaping hole in the center of her chest where the heavy-caliber slug had torn through her. A .52-caliber, judging by the size of the hole. The same caliber Fargo preferred. The same caliber Vic Dunn preferred.

The killer still lived, Fargo realized. Dunn was out there somewhere, stalking him. He wondered if Dunn had been aiming at him and hit Sym by mistake, but after reviewing his fight with her in his mind's eye he knew Dunn had shot her on purpose. She was on Dunn's list, after all. Still, Fargo would have expected Dunn to shoot him first, not her. Unless it was Dunn's way of throwing down a gauntlet, of letting him know Dunn was still alive and out for his hide.

Whatever, Fargo could no longer take his enemies for granted. He was up against a man every bit his equal and as bloodthirsty as they came. It would take all his skill, all his wits to survive this time.

Fargo stuck the Colt in his holster, cocked the Sharps, and rose high enough to scan the mountain. A gust of wind seemed to take his hat and fling it a dozen feet. Knowing better, he went prone, counting the seconds in his head. At the count of three he heard the shot. It told him that Dunn was over eight hundred yards away. To make matters worse, Dunn had the advantage of elevation.

Twisting, Fargo made for the woods to the east of the mill. He wasn't fool enough to get into a shooting match with a skilled marksman who held all the cards. Staying low until he was in the brush, Fargo rose. He could see his hat, but wasn't about to try and retrieve it, since Vic Dunn was waiting for him to do just that.

Hurrying to where he had left the Ovaro, Fargo mounted and swung to the north. He never left cover once as he rode clear around the valley to the mountain from which Vic Dunn had fired at him. Concealing the stallion in a stand of hemlock, he climbed the west slope of the mountain until he judged he was higher than Dunn must be. It had taken him over an hour but the labor was well worth it if he could put an end to Dunn once and for all.

Working his way down the mountain was a painstaking chore. Fargo had to constantly scour the brush on all sides, always alert for a hint of motion or the faintest of alien sounds, while at the same time he had to place each foot down with the utmost care. A single snapped twig would give him away. Even scraping against a tree trunk or boulder might do it if Dunn were close enough to hear.

About a third of the way down the mountain reared a cluster of gigantic boulders. Fargo suspected he would find Dunn there since the boulders offered not only a fine place to hide but a clear line of fire into the valley. Like a ghost he stalked among them, probing shadows and scaling a few flat boulders to see if Dunn had done the same.

In due course Fargo came to the lowest boulder and spotted a fresh footprint in the soft soil. In the hope Dunn was on top, he slowly climbed. The killer wasn't there, although a spent cartridge showed that he had been. Fargo knelt and searched the slope below, then happened to gaze toward the sawmill.

Vic Dunn sat astride the calico, close to Symphony's body.

The sunlight glinted off an object he held close to his face as he doffed his black hat and waved.

Fargo's blood boiled. The killer had played him for a green-horn, circling around to where he had been while he wasted his time trying to catch Dunn unawares. That glinting object, he knew, was a small telescope, or spyglass as some called them. It gave Dunn even more of an edge.

But this time Dunn had outsmarted himself. Fargo raised the Sharps and quickly adjusted the sight. He saw Dunn lower the hat and turn the calico, making for the nearest corner of the mill. There would only be time for one shot. Fargo aimed hastily, centered the bead, and fired just as Dunn reached the building. In his rush he failed to compensate for the wind and instead of taking Dunn's head off, he returned the favor Dunn had done him and blasted the black hat into the grass.

Vic Dunn disappeared. Fargo reloaded and waited to see if the killer would make a fight of it, but Dunn had too much sense to take the bait. Sliding down from the boulder, he jogged to the stallion, stepped into the stirrups, and trotted to the south. He had delayed long enough. With both Decker and Dunn on the loose, he had to find the Britches and the Harpers and see to their safety before he confronted the timber king and the professional killer for the final time.

Once off the mountain, Fargo went the length of the valley and turned to the southeast. Since Dunn might still be in the area, he rode with the Sharps across his lap. Soon he struck the trail left by the women and Jess and followed it due south. Within a mile he found where another rider had stumbled on the tracks and turned in the same direction.

Fargo guessed it had to be Decker, and he prodded the Ovaro into a lope. His cat and mouse with Dunn had taken so long, he'd given Decker plenty of time to overtake the Britches and their friends and do them in.

The tracks wound into the mountains, crossed an arid valley that lacked a stream, and up the slope of an L-shaped ridge dotted with madrones and lush with grass. The top afforded a sweeping vista of the countryside. It was an ideal spot to make camp, impossible for anyone to approach without being seen.

Fargo figured the women had planned to wait there for him, only now they were gone. A short search revealed where

Decker had snuck up on them as they rested on a long log. Their pistols and rifles lay in the grass. The tracks led down the shadowy slope on the other side, through pines and dense brush thick with poison oak, and finally to a meandering creek not more than four feet wide and four inches deep, lined with small ferns. They had crossed at a bend where a gravel bar gave their horses firm footing.

Beyond the creek, the land rose steeply to the top of a hill crowned with isolated red cedars. Fargo picked his way, the Sharps in his hands. He doubted that Decker would take them very far. Seconds later low voices confirmed it. They were right on top of the hill.

Fargo veered to the right, into a marshy area rife with high reeds. He saw a large snake slither from his path and was glad the Ovaro didn't nicker. Close timber bordered the marsh, many of the trees dead or dying. They posed a problem, since dead limbs snapped easier and louder than healthy ones. He brushed them aside with care and watched where the stallion placed its hooves.

A low spine covered with prickly briars flanked the hill. Fargo dismounted, tied the reins to a branch, and crept around the blackberry bushes and up through some thin oaks to a knob of earth big enough to hide behind. Rearing slowly to the top of the knob, he took in the scene before him.

Their horses had been tied to cedars. The women and Tune all sat in a row facing Abe Decker, who held a rifle on them. Jess Harper lay sprawled beside a madrone, a small pool of blood framing his head. It was impossible to tell whether he had been shot or clubbed.

Decker walked back and forth, smirking wickedly, enjoying his victory. "Well, this is the end of the line, ladies. We're far enough off the beaten path that no one will find your bodies for weeks, maybe months."

Maude held her chin high and said with contempt. "I always knew Sym did right by turning you down. You're as low as they come, Abraham. And they'll catch you and hang you eventually."

"Wrong, old woman," Decker said. He nodded at his horse. "I'm not as dumb as you seem to think I am. Can you guess what I have in my saddlebags?"

"I couldn't care less," Maude said.

"I'll tell you anyway, just so I can see the look on your face." Decker chuckled. "I have two Cayuse tomahawks and a Cayuse knife I aim to use to cut all of you up a little after I shoot you."

Prima, who had merely glared at the timber lord until now, burst out angrily, "You're going to try and pin the blame on the Indians!"

"And why not? It's no secret the Cayuse tribe hates whites. They killed that missionary couple, Marcus Whitman and his wife, a few years back, didn't they? So no one will think twice when they find evidence that Cayuse warriors were to blame for your deaths as well."

"You have this all thought out," Melody said in contempt.

Maude appeared puzzled. "If you had this planned from the beginning, why did you send for Vic Dunn? He doesn't come cheap, I hear. You could have killed us outright and spared yourself the expense."

Decker stopped pacing. "To tell you the truth, I didn't think I could do the job. I've shot a few men in my time, but never any women and children." He looked at the rifle in his hands and snorted. "And now look. I can do it, after all. It will be easy as pie."

Sky Fargo had heard enough. He stood, training the Sharps on Decker's back, and declared, "Not from where I stand. Set down the rifle and take a step back."

The timberman stiffened and started to turn, then hesitated. Decker nervously fingered his rifle while looking out of the corner of his eye at Fargo. "I might tie you," he blustered.

"Even if you do, you're dead."

Unexpectedly, Maude Britches jumped to her feet, stepped quickly forward, and tore the rifle from Decker's grasp before he made up his mind to resist. "You won't be needing this anymore, mister."

Prima was a step behind the matron. She snatched the timberman's six-gun out and pointed it at him. "Now what was that you were saying about cutting us up?"

Fargo walked over, roughly grabbed Decker by the arm, and shoved him to the ground. "Behave yourself while we decide what to do with you."

Decker licked his thin lips and looked from one to the other of them, his ferret features seamed with worry. "I won't let you turn me over to the law," he said. "I'd rather be shot than hung."

Maude wagged the rifle in front of his nose. "You don't have any say in the matter. Speaking for myself, I like the notion of watching you swing. I hear tell it's sheer hell when that old rope begins to tighten around your neck and you're flopping in the air with nothing under you except eternity."

Tune, Melody, and Prima ran to Jess and rolled him over. Fargo turned to see if there was anything he could do. The bleeding had stopped, but the left side of Jess's head, below a nasty gash, was caked with blood.

"Decker hit him for no reason," Prima said, holding back tears. "My boy was doing just like he was told, but Decker smashed him over the head anyway."

"We ought to do the same to that scum, then chop on him with his own tomahawks," Melody proposed. "See how he likes it!"

"I agree," Harmony chimed in. "Better yet, let's stick him down low with that Cayuse knife. Too bad Sym ain't here. She'd do it and laugh the whole while."

Maude half turned at the mention of her eldest. "Where is she, anyway? She should have caught up with us long ago. It isn't like her to be gone so long, not when she knows we're in trouble." She glanced at Skye. "Do you have any idea what happened to her?"

Fargo hated being the bearer of bad tidings. But before he could inform them of Sym's death, Abe Decker exploded into action, taking advantage of Maude's distraction to surge to his feet while at the same time he seized hold of the barrel of her rifle and swung it to the left. Maude, instead of letting go, tried to hold on and was flung into Fargo. They fell together, Maude's legs entangled in his.

Expecting Decker to blast them both, Fargo tried to raise the Sharps but Maude's flailing arm bumped it aside. He heard the *crack-crack* of two shots and shoved Maude off him, none too gently. Jumping up, he spotted Prima holding Decker's smoking pistol, then saw Decker himself just disappearing over the crest of the hill, on foot.

"I'll go after him," Fargo said, breaking into a sprint. He had gone but a few yards when Prima appeared at his elbow.

"You might need some help, and I owe the bastard for my Wes, and what he did to Jess."

There was no time to argue or Fargo would have. A cornered beast was always the most dangerous kind, and Decker would be desperate. At the crest he paused and dropped into a crouch, pulling her down beside him in case Decker tried to pick them off. A shot rocked the forest and the bullet buzzed overhead.

"Thanks," Prima said.

"Do both of us a favor and stay here," Fargo said.

"Would you if they were your sons?"

Reflecting that women had a lot of gall to claim men were more hardheaded, Fargo inched forward far enough to see the marsh and the creek. Decker was nowhere in sight, but Fargo felt positive the timberman was somewhere below, waiting for one of them to show themselves. "Stay down and fire a shot into those reeds every minute or so," he directed the redhead.

"Trying to keep me from being harmed?" Prima asked, sounding offended.

"I need someone to keep Decker occupied while I go on around," Fargo explained, and dashed off along the rim of the hill to forestall an argument. He didn't angle onto the slope until he was past the briars. The Ovaro looked at him but made no sound as he went by. Swinging wide of the dead trees, he came to the creek and halted.

Fargo scanned the reeds, seeking a telltale dark form. If Decker was there, he was well hidden. Fargo edged into the creek with the intention of getting closer to the marshy plot, and noticed the water flowing past his boots was discolored. Looking closer, he discovered the water coming from upstream had been muddied. He instantly figured out the reason and hurried upstream, setting his feet lightly so the water wouldn't splash.

The wily Decker was trying to lose them by relying on one of the oldest tricks in the book. By following the creek, he wouldn't leave prints. And if he found a rocky spot bordering the low bank, he could climb out with no one being the wiser.

Fargo glanced at the hill. Prima had seen him and started to rise. He motioned for her to stay down and increased his speed, trying to get out of sight before she took it into her pretty head to run down and join him. Putting an end to Decker would be chore enough without having to worry about her safety.

Then there was the matter of Vic Dunn. As sure as Fargo lived and breathed, the killer would show up sooner or later. Fargo wanted Decker taken care of beforehand so he could devote his full attention to Dunn.

The muddy water continued to flow by, which meant Decker was still in the creek. Fargo approached a bend and slowed. He had to be careful about his footing since there were countless smooth stones underfoot which could cause him to slip, as well as muddy stretches where he'd sink halfway to his knees. Bending down to see around a bush, he glimpsed Decker going around another bend thirty yards away.

Fargo hurried on, anxious to get close enough to draw a bead. He didn't count on Decker turning and looking back, yet that's what Decker did. The timber king cursed and snapped off two shots. Fargo dived for the right bank a fraction of a second before the first blast. He landed in dank grass as the rifle crashed again and the slug thudded into the mud next to him.

Decker spun and fled. Fargo gave chase, spraying water in all directions with every step. Stealth was no longer needed but common sense was. Rather than barge around the corner, Fargo stepped onto the left bank and cut directly across the finger of land around which the creek curled. He avoided more poison oak, vaulted a downed spruce, and saw Abe Decker fleeing madly up a rocky grade.

Loose pebbles cascaded from under the timberman's boots. Decker had to use his hands to scrabble to the top. Once there, he darted into the undergrowth with not so much as a backward glance.

Fargo ran to the bottom of the grade, then stopped. Doing as Decker had done invited a bullet to the brain if Decker was smart enough to be waiting for him. He circled to the left, to where the grade ended. A five-foot high gully pointed upward.

Fargo jumped to the bottom and worked his way higher. Decker was nowhere to be seen.

Saplings covered the slope above the grade, and there was enough thick brush to hide a small army. Fargo suspected that Decker had gone to ground somewhere in the maze of vegetation. He wasn't about to go in after him, not when there was an easier way. Halfway past the sapling he scaled the opposite side of the gully, then took up a position beside a pine. There were plenty of small rocks lying about. He picked up one, hefted it a few times, and threw it into the brush near the grade.

There was no reaction.

Fargo selected another rock. He hurled this one high and long, into the middle of the saplings. The rock hit one of the slender trees, bounced off into another, and fell into a thicket, making a lot of racket. Fargo was ready, yet once more Decker failed to show himself.

For the third time Fargo let a rock fly, this one higher than any of the others. It hit with a resounding smack, and hardly had it touched the ground than Abe Decker leaped up a score of feet from the spot and fired in that direction. Fargo centered the Sharps and called out, "Hey!"

The timber baron whirled. His mouth went wide with horror that changed to shock as Fargo's shot bored through his chest from front to back. Decker fell into the undergrowth, invisible except for a single foot that poked into the air as if pointing the way.

Fargo dashed into the gully and across to the saplings. The foot hadn't moved but he was taking no chances. He drew the Colt and kept it cocked until he saw the pie-sized red stain on Abe Decker's shirt and Decker's vacant eyes. "Finally," Fargo said aloud, and wheeled.

Jess Harper had recovered enough to sit with his back propped against a tree trunk and was drinking water from a tin cup when Fargo emerged from the woods. Prima and Maude hustled to meet him.

"Well?" they both asked at the same time.

Fargo nodded.

Maude let out a breath in relief and clasped her hands as if in prayer. "Hallelujah! It's over, then! Really over! He was the last of them."

"Not quite," Fargo corrected her. "Dunn is still alive."

"I thought you shot him?" Prima said.

"So did I. I guess his head is as hard as mine." Fargo recalled the bad tidings he had to relate, and did so, mentioning only how Symphony had died, not how she tried to bash in his skull.

The effect on Maude was predictable. She covered her mouth with a hand and uttered a choking sob. "My sweet Sym!" Maude's eyes brimmed with tears. "She was my firstborn, Mr. Fargo, and they're always special. Oh, God!" She turned to Prima, put her head on the redhead's shoulder, and bawled.

Fargo walked off as Harmony and Melody rushed over to learn why their mother was crying. He would rather they heard it from Maude, not him.

The Ovaro lifted its head at Fargo's approach. Weariness washed over him as he climbed into the saddle. He tried to remember when he had last had a good night's sleep and a hot meal. And a bath would be nice, he reflected, a long, hot soak to soothe all his aches and pains, not the least of which was the temple wound which had begun throbbing again. He rode down to the creek and splashed water on it, then soaked his bandanna and tied it around his head to keep the wound cool for a while. He missed having his hat and debated going back to the sawmill to reclaim it.

A shout from Prima Harper brought Fargo to the hilltop. "We've decided to leave right away," she informed him. "Jess needs doctoring and rest. Since my spread has been burned out, we're going to stay at Grizzly Gulch with Maude and the girls a spell."

"I'll go along in case Dunn shows," Fargo offered.

"We'd be grateful," Prima said, her tone implying she would be more than happy to show her appreciation in the same way she had the last time.

It took them the better part of the day to reach their destination. The women were more exhausted than Fargo; Melody and Harmony rode while dozing half the time. Jess Harper had to ride double with Tune, and he was so weak he sagged against her the whole ride.

Fargo had no choice but to stay fully alert. He paid particular attention to the high ridges and mountaintops since Dunn would go for the high ground. At times he felt as if unseen eyes were on them, and the skin between his shoulder blades would prickle. No shots punctuated the feeling, though. Which puzzled him. If Dunn was out there, what was he waiting for?

The little game Dunn had played at the old sawmill came to mind. Fargo imagined that the killer got a perverse sort of pleasure out of prolonging the suffering of his victims. Or maybe, he reasoned, Dunn just liked for them to worry awhile, to fray their nerves so they would be that much easier to kill. Vic Dunn was a natural born predator and wouldn't miss a trick.

There were squeals of delight from several of the women when the mouth of Grizzly Gulch at long last appeared. Maude trotted up beside Fargo and commented, "Home. I was beginning to think I'd never see it again." A cloud fell on her features. "It won't be the same without Leland. I doubt we can make ends meet without Sym and him to do the heavy work. I might have to sell out and take my girls back to Arkansas. Rear them proper, with schooling and church on Sundays."

"They'll love that," Fargo said dryly.

Maude chuckled. "I'll need to find some cotton to plug my ears or they'll wear me to a frazzle complaining." She glanced back. "They're wild as catamounts, I know, but deep down they're good girls. Tuney most of all. She deserves the chance to lead a good life."

Fargo couldn't help wondering how the girl would take to leaving Jess Harper. Knowing them, they'd probably elope to California. He faced Maude to tell her as much and saw the forehead of her horse erupt in a crimson geyser. The boom of the big Sharps reached them a moment later. Maude, petrified, just sat there as her mount keeled over and would have been pinned under it had Fargo not quickly leaned down, coiled an arm around her waist, and pulled her off. "Find cover!" he bellowed at the others, and galloped toward a boulder big enough to shield the Ovaro.

The others tried. Harmony reined to the right and made for

some trees but covered less than ten feet before the rifle boomed again and her horse went down, spilling her in the dust. Tune Britches cut her horse to the left and was almost to a patch of brush when the Sharps cracked a third time and the front legs of her horse buckled. She was pitched hard over the animal's shoulders and lay on her side, stunned. Jess Harper clawed at the saddle and was able to stay on. Not that it did him any good. The next second their mount toppled over. Jess tried to jump clear but in his weakened state he was too slow and his left leg wound up pinned.

Melody and Prima did reach cover, but Prima, on seeing her son's plight, promptly wheeled her horse and galloped to his rescue. She was halfway to him when the crash of the .52 brought her horse crashing to the earth. She scrambled to her feet and ran to Jess.

Fargo, safe behind the boulder, lowered Maude down and reached for his own Sharps. Judging by the shots, he knew that Vic Dunn was somewhere on top of Grizzly Gulch. He began to slide his rifle out, then stopped on hearing his name shouted from on high.

"You know who this is!" the killer went on. "I've got that pretty little filly in my sights, and if you don't do exactly as I say, she dies!"

Fargo looked at Tune, who groaned loudly but had yet to move. Dunn could put a slug into her without half trying.

"And after I blow her brains out, I'll pick off the boy and his mother!" Dunn went on. "I could have killed them all just now, but I needed them for leverage." He paused. "I'm going to count to ten. If you're not standing right out in the open by then, with your hands over your head, I start shooting them." He paused again. "Leave your Sharps. But I don't much care if you keep your pistol and that toothpick they say you carry. Neither will help you any."

All the women were looking at Fargo. "Don't do it," Maude said. "If you do, he'll gun you down."

"Not right away he won't," Fargo responded. "He wants to toy with me first, like a cat does with a mouse." Swinging off the stallion, he handed her the reins and strode from out of the boulder's shadow, his hands reaching for the sky as he'd been told to do.

Mocking laughter wafted from the north rim of the gulch. "I knew you were soft!" Dunn taunted. His laughter resumed, then his tone sobered. "Here is how we'll do it. I want you to walk on into the gulch. Just keep walking until I tell you to stop. And remember. Try to hide, try to turn and run back, try any tricks at all, and I'll kill the girl. So get moving!"

"Skye, no!" Prima called out. "We can get Tune to cover before he gets the range."

"He already has the range," Fargo reminded her as he headed toward the gulch. He lowered his arms and acted as calm as if he were strolling down a city street. Inwardly, his mind raced as he tried to think of a way to beat the killer at the killer's own game. The odds seemed hopeless. Dunn was high on top of the gulch, far out of normal pistol range. A highly skilled marksman could hit a man-sized target at fifty or even seventy-yards. Perhaps a handful of men in the whole country could drop an enemy at one hundred yards with a six-gun. But twice that distance? And almost straight up? Never in a million years could anyone make such a shot, which was why Dunn had let him keep the Colt. Dunn was rubbing it in to make him feel even more helpless.

Fargo looked back once and saw most of the women standing, a few wringing their hands. He smiled and went on, staying in the middle of the rutted track that led into the depths of the gulch. Above him low laughter sounded. Vic Dunn was enjoying himself immensely. Fargo halted and scanned the rim. Instantly the killer's Sharps banged and the bullet ripped into the dirt inches from his left foot.

"I didn't tell you to stop! Keep on going!"

Fargo did as he was told. He hadn't caught a glimpse of the killer but suspected Dunn was keeping pace with him as he went steadily deeper into the gulch. And that worked in his favor. Because once they were around the first bend, Dunn would be unable to see the women.

Fargo steeled his nerves and wondered how long it would be before Dunn decided to put a slug into him. To the right was the stream, bordered by large boulders. He walked another ten yards, and suddenly another shot sounded. Like before, the bullet missed by inches.

"That's far enough, Trailsman!" Dunn hollered. "It's the

160

end of the line for you. Try to make it interesting. See how long you can stay alive."

The words were no sooner out of the killer's mouth than Fargo darted toward the boulders. The big Sharps cracked, the shot clipping fringe off his buckskin shirt. Fargo reached a large slab of rock and ducked behind it as the sound of another shot rumbled off the gulch walls and the slug whined off the top of the slab. He drew the Colt and crouched down.

"Think hiding will help you?" Dunn shouted. "Watch and learn!"

The Sharps cracked again, and again. The slugs hit among the boulders and ricocheted wildly, one coming so close to Fargo that it nearly took off an ear. Fargo cocked the Colt, then straightened and snapped a shot at the rim. He wasn't trying to hit Dunn, and he hoped Dunn didn't realize that.

Harsh cackling erupted up above. Dunn was having a grand time at Fargo's expense. I gave you credit for more sense than that!" the killer roared. "You can't hit me with that belly gun from there. Here! Try again if you want!"

Fargo peeked out, and there stood Vic Dunn, perched on the edge of the cliff, his arms out from his sides, a broad smile creasing his face. Standing, Fargo raised the Colt. Dunn howled with mirth. But there was a fact the killer had forgotten. Sure, pistols were only reliable at short range, but they could shoot much farther. Everyone knew that firing one into the air was dangerous because the bullets sometimes flew half a mile or more. A lot of people had lost their lives when struck out of the blue by someone shooting a long ways off. Hunters had suffered the same fate.

Fargo hadn't forgotten, and he was staking his life on the knowledge. He aimed at Dunn's chest, then elevated the barrel another inch and a half to allow for the angle and the range. It would be sheer luck if he made the shot, but it was the only chance he had. He stroked the trigger.

Vic Dunn stood poised on the brink of the cliff a few moments longer, his grin unchanged, his posture relaxed. Then his knees bent, his arms drooped, the Sharps fell, and he seemed to dive into the air as if taking a plunge in a river. Halfway down he flipped over and plummeted feet first, falling straight as a rock until he hit the bottom of the gulch with a loud thud.

Fargo ran over. The killer's body had crumpled on impact into a miserable heap of shattered bones and pulp, all except Dunn's head, which was in one piece. Dunn still wore the stupid smile. And on his forehead above his eyes was a neat round hole.

"I'll be damned," Fargo said softly to himself. Turning, he hurried on out of the gulch to help the women. Once they were taken care of, he would mount up and head for California. And, he thought wryly, never again would he take a pistol for granted. He patted the Colt, shoved it into his holster, and ran out into the sunlight.

LOOKING FORWARD!
The following is the opening
section from the next novel in the exciting
Trailsman series from Signet:

**THE TRAILSMAN #162
REVENGE AT LOST CREEK**

*1860, the Montana territory,
a land guarding the secrets of men
and the riddle of greed . . .*

It was one of those times when the big man with the lake blue eyes wished his hearing was not so acute. He had been distinctly uneasy upon his arrival in this flea-bitten little town. He didn't need complications. He took another bite of the beef and bean sandwich on his plate as he sat in a corner of the saloon. The sandwich was good, the bourbon smooth, only the voices of the men on the other side of the thick wooden beam kept intruding.

"All we gotta do is screw her," the one said, a raspy voice. "Over and over. Hell, we can sure do that."

"I'm all for it. We can cut to see who does her first," another one said with a high-pitched guffaw.

"I'll bet she's a virgin. She's the kind, prim and prissy and all uptight. She won't recover for a year," a third voice said. "Never screwed a virgin before. I'll enjoy this."

"She's got the right name, too . . . Priscilla. I knew a Priscilla once. She was an uptight little bitch, too," a fourth man put in, a low, growly voice. "When do we do her?"

"What's the matter with tonight . . . later?" the raspy voice answered. "It'll be easy. It's not like she'll be at home with her pa guardin' her."

"Maybe we oughta think about it some more," the man with

the high voice responded. Fargo finished the last of his sandwich and downed the bourbon.

"Why? We just take her and do it," the raspy voice said.

"That's right," the one with the low growl chimed in. "I need to get laid, and a little uptight virgin will be extra perfect."

"Besides, it always helps to combine business with pleasure," the answer came and with it the high-pitched guffaw.

Fargo felt himself frowning at the remark, unclear how it fit. The waitress came over, took his money, and he rose and walked from the saloon, slowing to cast a quick glance at the four men around the table. They were huddled together, still laughing, thoroughly ordinary in appearance, though one sported a high-crowned black Stetson. Fargo walked on and stepped outside into the night air and walked to where the Ovaro was tied to the hitching post. He pushed away the conversation he'd overheard. He wasn't keeper of the town's morals. And he wasn't even certain the men hadn't just been bragging, hollow boasting based on wishful thinking. He'd seen that often enough, he reminded himself as he swung from the saddle and sent the magnificent horse with the jet-black fore and hind quarters and pure white section into the night.

He didn't need any more uncertainties, not on this strange undertaking. He had a tomorrow filled with them, and that was more than enough. Besides, all he had was a first name, Priscilla, and how was he going to track down a girl from just a first name? Damn, he swore. The damn conversation insisted on sticking in him, and he made a face as he pulled to a halt. He swore again. Someone had once told him that a conscience was the worst burden to put on a man. They were right, he grimaced as he turned the Ovaro around. He had to give it a try, if only for his own peace of mind. But it could be the proverbial needle in a haystack, he realized and decided he had only one thing to go on: where *not* to look.

If this girl was as they had described her, he could cross out the dance hall and the local bordello. But that left God knows how many houses and farms in and around town. But his brow creased as something one of the men said worked its way through his mind. *It'll be easy. It won't be like she's got a pa guarding her.* That said she probably wasn't a part of one of the families in the area, and he spurred the Ovaro back to town. The town was a scroungy place, but it had a bank, a church, and a clapboard house that put itself forward as an inn. He had glimpsed all three when he'd ridden into town but a few hours earlier, and he drew up before the building with the small sign that proclaimed: CYPRESS INN.

He dismounted and walked into a dimly lit foyer, a public room with tables and chairs to one side and across from it, a desk and a counter where the desk register lay closed. A sallow-faced kid rose from behind the desk, stepped to the counter, and surveyed him with bored indifference. "Need a room?" he asked.

"No. Need some information. You have a young woman named Priscilla staying here?" Fargo answered.

"We don't go by first names," the youth said curtly.

"I suppose not, but I'd guess you don't have too many young women staying here. A look at the register might tell me what I want to know," Fargo said.

"We don't give out our guests' names," the youth snapped. Fargo's glance went across the entranceway, took in the peeling paint, frayed curtains, and a stuffed chair with torn upholstery.

"I'm sure this is a very high-class operation, but I'm asking you to make an exception. It's for the young lady's good," Fargo said.

"Can't do it," the youth said, a crafty insolence coming into his eyes.

"Would a little offering persuade you to change your mind, say a gold dollar?" Fargo asked mildly.

"It might," the youth said.

Fargo's smile was pure affableness. The youth's mouth dropped open as a big hand was suddenly around his throat, the revolver pressed against his temple. "Then this ought to persuade you, too," Fargo said. "Open the goddamn register." The youth, now ashen-faced, opened the gray-covered register book with one hand, and Fargo released his grip and pulled the

Colt back. "That's much more cooperative," Fargo said and let his eyes go down the page of the register. There weren't that many names, and his finger came to rest at one. "I'll be dammed," he murmured. "Priscilla Dale." He lifted his eyes to the youth.

"Room four . . . end of the hallway," the youth said.

"How long has she been here?" Fargo asked.

"Two days," he was told.

"Thanks for your help," Fargo said, holstering the Colt. The youth closed the register without looking up, and Fargo walked down a long hallway to the dim end where he found the door and knocked. He had to wait only a few moments before the door was opened and he saw the young woman, a blue-gray robe concealing most of her figure. "Priscilla Dale?" he asked.

"Yes," she said.

He took in a very young face, pretty in a fresh, scrubbed way. Ash blond hair had been pulled up atop her head, for bed, he supposed, and he saw eyebrows to match her hair. She was smooth-skinned and pale, with very round, very wide eyes that helped give her a little-girl appearance, a small nose and a small mouth held more primly than lips ought to be held. Yet her light blue eyes held a cool, contained appraisal that was very adult.

"The name's Fargo . . . Skye Fargo. I heard some men talking about you in the saloon," he said.

Her wide eyes grew wider. "Talking about me?"

"Unless there's another Priscilla Dale in town," Fargo said.

"I doubt that," the young woman said.

"Me, too," Fargo agreed.

"Who were these men?" Priscilla Dale asked.

"Town loafers, I'd guess. I didn't get names."

"What were they saying?"

Fargo felt the moment of uncomfortableness poke at him as he sought a less crude way of putting it than the four men had used. "They said they were going to take you," he offered.

"Take me?" she frowned.

"Enjoy you. Pleasure themselves with you. You want me to be plainer, honey?" Fargo said.

"No, that won't be necessary. I think I quite understand," Priscilla Dale said. "But I think you must have misunderstood whatever you heard."

"There was nothing to misunderstand," Fargo grunted.

"You must have. It's just ridiculous. I don't even know anyone in town. Why should they pick on me?" she said.

"Guess you took their fancy," Fargo said.

The very round light blue eyes stayed cool as she studied his chiseled handsomeness. "And what do you suggest?" she asked.

"I could take you out of here, or stay here with you," Fargo said.

"Absolutely not," Priscilla Dale snapped. "I don't mean to sound ungracious, but I'm not going off with a total stranger or have one stay in my room. That's out of the question."

"You think I've come here to make my own move on you?" Fargo questioned.

"Frankly, I don't know what to think," she said coolly. "Let's say whatever you heard you heard wrong. I think that would be the most charitable explanation I can give."

Fargo felt irritation stab at him. She was a snippy, suspicious little thing, her wide-eyed little-girl appearance cloaking a very unyielding stiffness. Prim, he grunted silently. The lowlifes at the saloon had been right about that. "I've said my piece, honey. You take it from here," he told her.

"Thank you for coming," she said, very proper dismissal in her tone as she closed the door.

"Sure thing," Fargo snapped as he strode down the hallway and out to where the Ovaro waited. He swung into the saddle and sent the Ovaro from the town at a fast canter, finally turned from the road and went up a low slope to a stand of boxelder and refused to wonder why he was so annoyed. He'd told her, warned her. He'd done his duty by her. His conscience was clear now. Hell, what more could anyone ask?

He found a spot to halt and dismounted, pulled down his bedroll and undressed and lay back. But he found sleep an uncooperative companion as he tossed and turned and pressed his eyes shut. He had no idea how long he wrestled with the night when he finally sat up, pulling his eyes open. "Ah, shit," he swore. "Goddamn stubborn, suspicious little package." It was only logic and reason pushing at him, he told himself, but he knew it was more. Conscience refused to be dismissed. It clung, like a wet leaf on a rock. Maybe it had been too much to expect her to take his offer, or believe his story about the men at the saloon. After all, as she'd said, he was a total stranger to her.

Maybe he'd been too quick to walk away from her. "Damn," he swore as he yanked on clothes and climbed onto the pinto. He set off at a gallop as he retraced steps back to the town. Slowing when he reached the inn, he reined to a halt in the still darkness and peered through the front entrance. He saw the youth asleep, head on his arms folded atop the desk, and he dismounted and entered the hotel on silent steps. Reaching the end of the hallway, he knocked on the door. There was no answer and he knocked again, then again, harder. There was still no answer and he tried the door. It was locked and his mouth was a tight line as he ran down the hall and outside, where he raced around to the back of the inn. He saw the open window at once and knew its grim meaning. They had been there. His eyes flicked to the ground.

The moon was nearly full, the hoofprints clear in the earth. He took a moment to kneel down and run his fingers over the prints. They hadn't more than a few minutes' start, the indented places still very warm and moist. He was on the Ovaro seconds later, following the trail of hoofprints. The four men had ridden across a field, the prints easy to follow, and he saw them go over a small dip and into a line of woods, mostly hackberry. He slowed as he spotted a light first, then a small house set back in the woods. He heard the sound of the men first, their voices loud, some slurred by liquor, and he dropped to the ground and moved to the house. They had left the door open and Fargo moved to where he could partly see into the single room.

One of the men came into view, thin, with a loose shirt and

torn Levi's, then the one with the high-crowned black hat. He found Priscilla Dale next, seated in a straight-backed chair, her knees held tightly together. They had pulled the robe from her, but she had on bloomers that fitted tightly around her legs and a camisole-like top that left her arms and shoulders bare. He saw fear in her eyes but also a cold contempt. The one with the black hat walked to her, and Fargo heard the other two men but they were out of his line of vision. With a quick motion the man seized her, pulled her arms over her head. "Take off her bloomers, Jake," he said. "It's time we got some of this brand-new pussy."

"Scum. Rotten scum," Priscilla Dale spat out as she kicked at the second man, who grabbed for her legs. Fargo heard the other two, still unseen, guffaw. The torn Levi's caught hold of her one leg, twisted, and Priscilla Dale cried out in pain. Fargo swore under his breath. He didn't want a bloodbath, especially when it might be Priscilla's. The black-hatted one would immediately use the young woman as a shield once he fired, Fargo realized, and the others would dive for the corners of the room out of his line of fire. That would still leave Priscilla trapped inside the house, still their hostage, and they'd know he was outside. He grimaced as he knew he had to make his first shot count for more than that.

He had to let it give Priscilla a chance to get out and cut down the odds some. His glance went to the kerosene lamp on the floor. He could shoot it out, he calculated, but would Priscilla think fast enough to get out or would she freeze in fright? He had to take the chance, he decided. He hadn't that many options open to him. Raising the Colt, Fargo took aim and fired. The black-hatted man shouted in pain as he fell backward, one hand clasping his shoulder. Fargo had already shifted the Colt and fired again, and the room was plunged into darkness as the lamp shattered. "Run for it," Fargo shouted over the surprised curses that rose, and he dropped low as a shot whistled through the doorway.

He glimpsed Priscilla half crawling, half flinging herself forward, white bloomers a flash in the darkness. She was at the doorway and he started to reach for her when three more shots came through the doorway and grazed his head. He dropped flat and saw the young woman being pulled back into the house, trying to kick herself free but failing. Fargo rolled and came up on one knee against the edge of the doorjamb, cursing softly. It had failed. The girl was still their hostage. He heard muttered exchanges from inside the house, a sharp cry of pain from Priscilla as she was pushed into a corner. "Let the girl go. That's all I want," he called.

A moment of muttering followed. "Let her go?" a voice called back. "We'll put a bullet through her."

"Do that and you're dead men. Guaranteed," Fargo said.

"You going to rush us, you dumb bastard?" the voice said with a sneer.

"Nope. I'm going to wait for morning," Fargo answered.

Fargo heard the surge of muffled voices as they realized the advantage would swing with the dawn, when he'd be able to pick them off as they tried to get out. He drew back from the edge of the doorway, reloaded the Colt, and rested on one knee. A voice came from inside the house. "Who the hell are you, mister?" it asked.

"Somebody who wants the girl," Fargo called back.

"She your woman?" the growly voice asked.

"She's not yours. That's all that matters," Fargo said.

"Let's talk about this. Step out where we can see you," another voice said.

"You boys have a real sense of humour," Fargo returned.

"You won't think it funny when you're dead," the man said.

"I'd guess it'll be dawn in about two hours," Fargo said, his voice casual as he rose to his feet. They were small-time. They hadn't the discipline to see it through. They'd try to make their way out, and he had to be ready when they did. He moved from alongside the doorway to the corner of the house, where he went to the rear. There was but one side window, too small to crawl through. Their only way out was through the front door, and he allowed himself a moment of grim satisfaction as he moved into the edge of the trees before the front of the house.

Settling down on one knee, he prepared to wait but found he

only had a half hour of waiting when the growly voice called out. "Bert's bleeding bad from where you got him," the man said. "We've got to get a doc for him." Fargo didn't answer. "You hear me?" the man asked. Fargo remained silent and listened to the muffled voices from inside the house. In moments the voice called out again. "You gonna answer us?" it asked. Fargo remained silent and heard more hasty exchanges. Finally, the growly voiced man spoke up again. "We're coming out to get a doc and we're taking her with us. You make one wrong move and she's dead, you hear me?"

Once more Fargo remained absolutely silent. They were dripping perspiration by now, he knew, their trigger fingers slippery. He stayed unmoving, hardly drawing a breath, his eyes on the doorway. The figures began to edge out, three of them, surrounding and holding Priscilla between them. They had left Bert behind, ostensibly to wait for them to fetch the doc. But he was probably waiting, watching from inside for Fargo to show himself. They were neither smart nor courageous, but they had a rodent-like caginess. He couldn't afford to take any chances, and he flattened himself on the ground, stretched out his arm, and took aim.

The one with the black hat had the gun against Priscilla's throat, the other two huddled beside her. Fargo let them turn for a moment, saw them sweep the trees in front of the house with long, nervous glances as they edged toward the horses at the far corner of the cleared space. He knew he could give them no more room. They'd shoot Priscilla out of fear or nervousness or just plain small-time meanness. His finger tightened on the trigger, and the shot exploded in the night. The high-crowned black hat flew from the man's head as he pitched forward. Fargo heard Priscilla's scream as the other two turned. One crumpled to the ground as Fargo's next shot exploded. The third one had gone into a crouch, and he was firing wildly into the trees until Fargo's shot cut him down.

Priscilla Dale had flung herself to the ground, and Fargo stayed motionless, his eyes on the house. "It's over. Come out," he called and waited. The figure appeared after a long moment, edging from the door, one shoulder bandaged but a gun still in his hand. "Bad idea that didn't work," Fargo said as he rose to his feet. "Drop the gun." The man let the gun slide from his hand, and Fargo stepped forward and kicked the weapon aside. "Get out of here," he said. "Before I change my mind." The man started toward the horses, walking slowly, and Fargo took Priscilla Dale by the arm. He was steering her to where the Ovaro waited when he heard a sound, the rustle of a shirtsleeve against leather. "Down," he yelled as he flung himself forward with her face forward, and the two shots grazed his head.

He rolled, heard the third shot thud into the ground, and then he was firing, three shots that blended together almost as one and the man slumped to the ground. The gun in his hand, a pocket pistol he'd pulled from inside his belt, fell from his fingers as he lay still. "My God," he heard Priscilla gasp, and she came to him again as he pushed to his feet, fingers digging into his arms.

"Stupid men do stupid things," Fargo said as he started to walk to the Ovaro, but she turned from him.

"I want to get my robe," she said and hurried into the house. She reappeared in moments, the blue-gray robe pulled tightly around her. He helped her into the saddle in front of him and rode slowly back to town. He felt the slenderness of her inside his arms as he held the reins. But her rear, pressed back into his crotch, had a very soft roundness to it. "There's no way I can thank you," she said as they rode. "I was very wrong not to listen to you."

"Can't blame you all that much," he said.

"I still don't understand any of it. I didn't know those men. I certainly didn't encourage them. I've only been here two days," she said.

"What brought you to Cypress?" Fargo asked.

"I came to meet some people. I arrived a few days early. But, as you said, they just took a fancy to me," Priscilla mused aloud.

"Probably," Fargo said, and she turned in the saddle to look at him with her round, wide eyes.

"What does that mean?" she asked.

"They said some things that stick with me," he answered.

"Such as?"

"For one thing, they knew you were at the inn," he said.

"I don't suppose it'd be hard to have learned that," Priscilla Dale said. "They probably know all the town girls."

"True enough," Fargo agreed. "But then they said something about combining business with pleasure."

The light blue eyes stayed on him, a furrow creasing her smooth forehead. "I certainly can't imagine what that meant," she said.

"It could've meant somebody paid them to take you," Fargo ventured, and her frown deepened.

"Nonsense. I don't have any enemies," Priscilla Dale said.

"Sometimes we have enemies we don't know about," Fargo remarked as he halted in front of the inn. She was still frowning, rejecting his answer, as he helped her from the Ovaro, his hands almost encircling the very small waist.

"Again, I've no way to thank you," Priscilla Dale said, standing before him. "It was a wonderful thing to do, and I'll be forever grateful to you for it." She pushed her hand out, shook his with a firm grip, and he smiled inwardly. One word flew into his mind: proper. She was being properly grateful. Not warmly, not spontaneously, not affectionately, but properly. Priscilla Dale was all properness. He doubted she'd ever done anything that was not proper. Proper and prim, he had to admit. Her voice cut into his thoughts. "Perhaps we'll meet again sometime and I'll be able to do something wonderful for you," she said. "Though I can't imagine what it might be," she added thoughtfully.

"You never know," Fargo said.

"Thank you again," she said, withdrawing her hand, and he half expected her to curtsy. But she turned and walked quickly into the inn. Fargo sent the Ovaro on at a walk and let himself feel good. Hell, good deeds were supposed to make you feel good, he murmured. God knows what he'd be feeling come tomorrow, he reminded himself.

⊘ SIGNET

THE TRAILSMAN— HAS GUN, WILL TRAVEL

☐ **THE TRAILSMAN #142: GOLDEN BULLETS by Jon Sharpe.** Skye Fargo goes on a Black Hills, South Dakota sleigh ride where he will have to do a lot of digging to uncover the truth about who killed who and why—and a lot of shooting to keep him from being buried with it.
(177533—$3.50)

☐ **THE TRAILSMAN #143: DEATHBLOW TRAIL by Jon Sharpe.** Skye Fargo has a gunhand full of trouble when an Arizona gold vein gushes blood.
(177541—$3.50)

☐ **THE TRAILSMAN #144: ABILENE AMBUSH by Jon Sharpe.** Skye Fargo was looking for rest and relaxation in Abilene, Kansas. What he found was five toothsome females who wanted to lead them over the plains in a couple of creaking wagons.... Skye said no, but the trouble was these lovely women wouldn't take no for an answer ... and they were willing to do anything short of telling the truth about the danger they were running from.
(177568—$3.50)

☐ **THE TRAILSMAN #145: CHEYENNE CROSSFIRE by Jon Sharpe.** Skye Fargo ... in the tightest spot in his life ... playing his most dangerous role ... a man who everyone thought was a monstrous murderer ... with his life riding on his trigger finger and a woman's trust ... Skye Fargo fights a Wyoming frame-up with flaming fury and blazing firepower.
(177576—$3.50)

☐ **THE TRAILSMAN #146: NEBRASKA NIGHTMARE by Jon Sharpe.** The settlers thought they had found a piece of paradise in the Nebraska Territory near the River Platte. But the trouble was ... a cougar named Nightmare, who killed without warning ... and a gang led by Rascomb.... What the farmers needed was a man who could kill a killer cat and outgun ... marauding murderers.... They got what they needed and more in Skye Fargo.
(17876—$3.50)

Prices slightly higher in Canada

Buy them at your local bookstore or use this convenient coupon for ordering.

PENGUIN USA
P.O. Box 999 – Dept. #17109
Bergenfield, New Jersey 07621

Please send me the books I have checked above.
I am enclosing $_____ (please add $2.00 to cover postage and handling).
Send check or money order (no cash or C.O.D.'s) or charge by Mastercard or VISA (with a $15.00 minimum). Prices and numbers are subject to change without notice.

Card #_____ Exp. Date _____
Signature_____
Name_____
Address_____
City _____ State _____ Zip Code _____

For faster service when ordering by credit card call **1-800-253-6476**

Allow a minimum of 4-6 weeks for delivery. This offer is subject to change without notice.